THE LAST DAYS OF THUNDER CHILD

Victorian Britain in Chaos!

C. A. Powell

ISBN: 9781484088265

Tribute to the Ironclad of H.G.Wells' *WAR OF THE WORLDS*

June: 1898

They really came, and this is the alternative history of that coming. Let us join the crew of *HMS Thunder Child* as she prepares to embark upon her doomed voyage—before her demise in courageous battle with three Martian tripods on the River Blackwater in Essex.

First story of Victorian Britain during the Martian apocalypse.

To my four sons; Lloyd, Paul, Robbie and Ryan

TABLE OF CONTENTS

CHAPTER 1

EMBARKATION AMID RUMOURS

Above the quay where the ironclad was moored, seagulls swooped and squealed in the June afternoon sky. It was as though the birds knew the vessel was about to embark across the shimmering swell, sparkling from sunbeams that burst with moments of brilliance. A sudden breeze swept brusquely across the bay—a surge that died as quickly as it had come. It caused the assembled crew to almost stiffen to attention without the order being given. They held themselves in check, standing at ease before the fluttering ensign—a Union Jack in the top corner of a Saint George's Cross.

Each man was in his own section. Sailors, stewards and stokers standing in neat rows behind their leaders. All uniforms had been thoroughly cleaned of the coal dust, as was the deck. Everywhere seemed to have been smothered the day before, when all had been ordered to bring the coal aboard. The rest of the day had been dedicated to cleaning the ship from top to bottom.

The crew wore summer dress, and had been brought on parade at the recessed quarterdeck. Before them was the main deck, horseshoe-shaped by the quarterdeck's lull, with a central stairway leading up to an array of officers who stood beneath two mounted guns on a revolving turret. The stubby muzzle-loading barrels barely protruding from the turret's gun ports. But then, *Thunder Child* was outdated by current Royal Navy standards. She still displayed an elegant power, as though aware of her past service to Queen Victoria's Royal Navy.

Such wonders were enough to hearten the spirits of Boy Seaman First Class Perry as he watched the higher ranks beneath the aft gun, waiting to welcome the new captain, who was rumoured to be an agreeable and sturdy Scottish fellow.

Perry had just arrived from the training ship *HMS Ganges*, where he had endured a year of harsh discipline. The excitement of his new posting added to his keen spirit, and although ships made of iron had been about for many years, he was pleased when passing civilians stopped in inquisitive groups to look in wonder at the vessel.

HMS Thunder Child was a mighty little ironclad indeed and at twenty-four years of age, having been completed in 1875, she was ready to be scrapped. However, she had won a momentary reprieve. Why? No one knew and Perry was confused when he arrived aboard a ship where the crew couldn't make out why he'd been sent. Not when her last voyage was for the breakers yard.

"Hope he gets here soon," whispered Jolly, careful not to be spotted.

"Jolly, report to the quartermaster afterwards," Chief Boatswain Pickles' voice boomed from behind. The man had a knack of being in the right place at the wrong time where insubordinates were concerned.

Perry froze, hoping he wouldn't be included in the punishment and gave a sigh of relief as the boatswain's mate began piping the side and the stamp to attention of the entire crew followed—a single figure of discipline.

All watched as the resplendent and handsome Captain McIntosh stepped aboard and allowed the whistle to fade. The new captain stood waiting for the ceremony to commence, and seemed pleased by the sturdy appearance of the crew waiting to greet him—confident he would get along with such fine men, knowing he could get the best from them.

They went through the time-honoured tradition of handing command to the captain, and when the formalities were concluded, he addressed the crew.

Perry, like many of the sailors, took an instant liking to the man. There seemed to be an aura about him. He was in his mid-thirties, neatly cut black hair, clean-shaven and uniform immaculate. When he spoke, it was with a confident Edinburgh accent.

"It gladdens me to stand before such a fine-looking crew, and it is with great pride and pleasure that I accept the command of *HMS Thunder Child*. I have received fresh orders as to our new voyage, which is, of course, not the original destination we had planned. You will all know more in due course, but in the meantime we shall put to sea immediately. Thank you."

He went off with the ship's officers, leaving the crew to fall out and attend their duties.

"Why do you think we're going somewhere else?" asked Jolly, as the crew began to fall out and go about their functions.

"I don't know." Perry was bewildered. "First I've heard."

"Well if you ask me, it doesn't sound too good. I'm not one for a rumour, but…"

"Jolly!" yelled Boatswain Pickles.

"Oh no," muttered Jolly. "Yes, Bosun".

The boatswain stood rigid—his angry face looked as though it would explode. Ginger side-burns clung to his flushed skin like wild red ivy, meeting a huge ginger moustache and full grown beard. He was the very picture of Victorian value. "Run along now, lad. The quartermaster will make sure you don't talk on parade. He is with the Supply Officer in the stores room. By God, boy, he'll teach a trumped-up little guttersnipe like you how to behave, so help me God he will. Now move."

"Yes, Bosun," yelled Jolly, running to the hatch and into the companionways that would lead to the stores, not daring to walk, even when out of the boatswain's sight.

Perry watched him go, then looked to Pickles, who was staring straight back at him. He averted his gaze and was about to leave, when he was yelled at too.

"Boy Seaman Perry, stop there now."

He froze to attention while Pickles moved forward. "Talking to you was he, boy?"

"Who, Bosun? Jolly?"

"Don't play smart with me, boy," he whispered, then yelled and Perry almost flinched expecting to be struck—which had happened on the odd occasion at the training school. "You know exactly who I mean. Never in all my life have I heard such drivel. Follow him now and when you get there, tell the quartermaster you're a little smart-ass and you need it knocked out of you. Now! Tell me what you say to the quartermaster, boy."

"I'm a little smart-ass and I need it knocked out of me, Bosun."

"Good. Run along then, there's a good chap."

Perry made off while the boatswain went about his business with a spring in his step, muttering to himself. "No one makes a horse's ass out of Chief Boatswain Albert Sydney Pickles." To him, the clear day with its serene sea held a surety that the coming voyage would be a good one, and certain in this belief, he indulged himself with a pause to look across the bay at some of the other vessels. During his years of service, he had seen and done a great many things, never once regretting his time in Her Majesty's Navy—although he often cursed the force, he never meant a word of it. He sighed, put his hands against his lapels and strode off with great aplomb.

Cursing his luck while making his way along the companionway, Perry knew the worst was yet to come. He was sure Bosun Pickles and Quartermaster Middleton had a scheme going to handle disorderly sailors, or at least those they decided were disorderly. He knocked at the stores room, entered, and was greeted by the sight of the quartermaster, whose appearance was very much like Bosun Pickles, except that his whiskers and beard were brown with touches of grey. He was booming at the top of his voice at Jolly, who was standing at attention, receiving a thorough dressing-down. The Supply Officer was nowhere in sight.

"I don't know what this blooming navy is coming to, boy. When some little upstart like you comes along and thinks he can go about making his own rules. It won't do, lad. Do you hear? It just won't do at all."

"No, Quartermaster," replied Jolly. Jolly had told the quartermaster what he had done and had left nothing out, as he was sure Boatswain Pickles would throw further light on the matter when they were next in the mess drinking together.

The quartermaster looked to Perry. "What are you here for, lad?"

"The Bosun says I'm to report to you for being a smart-ass and that I need it knocked out of me, Quartermaster."

Middleton's chest cavity filled with hot air and it was hard to tell whether he was angry, or secretly pleased to have another urchin to deal with. "Did he now? Well, you may be very pleased to know that dealing with little smart-asses is a speciality of mine, lad, so don't worry. I'll knock it out of you good and proper. God help you, boy, I will." He took a step back to look at both his sacrificial offerings. "Well this is cosy, isn't it?"

"Yes, Quartermaster," replied Perry and Jolly.

Middleton brought his hands together with a thunderous clap and Perry realised that the man was indeed, enjoying himself. "Well," he began. "Jolly I know, but you, lad, are one of the new boys. What's the name then?"

"It's Perry, Quartermaster. I arrived two days ago, sir."

"Did you, now?" Middleton liked saying 'Did you, now' or 'Is it, now'. Perry had heard the other sailors doing impressions of the man during light-hearted moments when resting. Things were a lot more sinister when confronting him.

"Yes, Quartermaster."

"What school, Boy Perry?"

"*HMS Ganges*, Quartermaster."

"Are you, now, and you come trotting along as a smart-ass in the hope that serving aboard *Thunder Child*, we would make you a more honourable young man? Is this not so, lad?" He began to walk behind Perry, who was trembling, knowing Middleton was playing games. The young sailor knew he would have to go through the routine of saying 'Yes' to everything.

"Yes, Quartermaster," he confirmed.

"Well now, isn't this jolly?"

"Pardon, Quartermaster?" asked Ordinary Seaman Jolly.

"Shut your mouth and talk when you're spoken to, Jolly. You can't make mistakes for having a silly name. There's no excuse for it, lad. Did you hear? No excuse."

"Yes, Quartermaster." Jolly then shut up, hoping Middleton would resume his interest in Perry. He wasn't disappointed.

"Well now, young Perry. What should we do with you—who have the keenness to become an upright British boy, who can serve his Queen and country? You do love your Queen, don't you, boy?"

"Yes, Quartermaster."

"And you do love your country?"

"Yes, Quartermaster."

"And you would be most grateful to any of the Queen's men who try to put you straight on matters of correction, wouldn't you, boy?"

"Yes, Quartermaster."

"So." He clapped his hands again and began rubbing them brusquely. "Any harsh punishment I administer is done for your benefit, young man. It makes sure you function at a high standard while aboard this ship. It will make a good and upright citizen of you when you go forth into the fearfulness of Civvy Street. Therefore, you will be grateful for the punishment I'm about to bring upon you, won't you, lad?"

"Yes, Quartermaster."

"Not much conviction in that one, boy. Let's have it with a bit of gusto now, come on, lad."

"Yes, Quartermaster," bellowed Perry, wanting to get on with it.

"Well now. Aren't you a most splendid young sailor indeed? I've got a lot of time for a reluctant smart-ass who is determined to shake off his stupidity by doing lots of fatigues. All the time in the blooming world, boy."

Perry stared back; unsure whether he was meant to respond, when Middleton stopped talking as though waiting for him to say something. "Y-Yes, Quartermaster."

"Right, you and Jolly follow me then. The Supply Officer has allowed for me to take such liberties with the stores."

He led them through a hatchway into another cabin with a counter halfway across the room. Behind it was another hatch leading to the stores, with shelves full of clothing and other supplies necessary for running a ship. He lifted a hinged part of the counter and smiled like Father Christmas allowing two boys into his grotto. "Well now, mustn't keep you likely lads waiting, must we? In you jolly well go."

"Pardon, Quarter…?" Jolly clenched his teeth, realising he had made the same mistake again.

"Shut your blooming mouth and speak when you're spoken to, Jolly. I've told you not to confuse your stupid name with that exquisite word I like to use in light-hearted discourse. Now you want to buck your blooming ideas up, lad, because you and me are going to fall out bloody big time. Do you understand?"

"Sorry, Quartermaster," replied Jolly.

"Are you, lad?" He acted like a poor, wretched man that was delighted by a new ray of hope. "Are you really sorry, lad?"

"Yes, Quartermaster." Now Jolly began to worry, knowing he had to walk the path Middleton was laying before him. The quartermaster clenched his fist and stared intently at him, as crocodile tears oozed from his wicked eyes—pretending to be overcome by the emotion of it all and like some stage-struck thespian, he played to his audience. "You mean you don't want to be a little guttersnipe who likes to make up his own rules anymore and you don't want to confuse your stupid name with my exquisite word I like to use in buoyant chit-chat?"

"No, Quartermaster."

He shook his head, overcome by the joy of it all. "Glory be, Jolly. You can make me a very proud man. You know that, don't you, boy?"

"Yes, Quartermaster." Jolly was beginning to get very worked up inside and wondered how such a devious and vindictive sod ever got to be born. He just wanted to do his punishment and get out of his evil sight. Oh, how he wished he'd not behaved so stupidly during the boarding parade.

"You do want it stamped out of you, don't you, boy?" said Middleton, as though his lamb might be tricking him.

"Yes, Quartermaster." Jolly wanted to scream with rage as he fought back the tears. How he would love to smash his fist in the quartermaster's face, but it was more than he dared do. The dialogue he was permitted made him feel even more uncomfortable, and he was convinced joining the navy was the absolute monster of mistakes if you were a regular chatterbox used to winning alehouse arguments with flippant banter. Jolly regarded himself as a very sharp fellow indeed, and these boatswains and quartermasters had an unfair advantage in Her Majesty's Navy, where rules allowed them to say what they pleased to men in his position.

"Right then, lad," he whispered benevolently, as though doing Jolly a good turn. He pointed to the buckets and mops. "Take those and grab one of the medium soap powders."

"Yes, Quartermaster." Jolly jumped to the task happy to be out of the man's way, even for a moment.

"Well now, Perry." The thespian was back with a new enthusiastic persona.

Perry, who felt no sense of privilege from the performance, played the game according to Middleton's rules. "Yes, Quartermaster."

"That box, lad—up there. It's full of old toothbrushes. Go and fetch them."

He complied, then stood awaiting the next set of instructions.

"Follow me then." The beam on his big, cherubic face could not help but agitate them as they followed Middleton along companionways towards the aft, where the officers were quartered. They were presented to the chief steward—a tall, lean Irishman with a sharp chin and pointed nose. His eyes were small slits, from which shone the piercing blue of his irises.

"Chief Steward Doherty. Two enthusiastic lads for you."

The steward gazed down at them. There was no sign of humour in his features, just a cold stare.

"You do want it knocked out of you, don't you, lads?" said Quartermaster Middleton again.

"Yes, Quartermaster," they replied.

"And for what you are about to receive, you will be truly grateful?"

"Yes, Quartermaster." They spoke as one.

"Well, where's the thanks then?"

"Thank you, Quartermaster." Their voices were demoralised, accepting the inevitable.

Middleton frowned. "Bit more gusto, lads."

"Thank you, Quartermaster," they shouted.

"Good. Well now." He brought his hands together with a thunderous clap and began rubbing them briskly, as though bubbling with enthusiasm. "Chief Steward Doherty here has a few little jobs for you in the officers' ablutions. Lots of intricate scrubbing and cleaning."

A reluctant display of humour disfigured Doherty's face—he knew Middleton of old. Secretly, he sympathised with the young lads who received the punishment detail, but then it had happened to all of them in the past, and he decided to play along with the quartermaster.

"Well," he said in his mild, West Irish accent. "I would be most grateful if you would bring these lively looking lads this way please."

"My pleasure, Chief Steward Doherty. Come along, lads. Mustn't keep the officers waiting for their nice clean toilets, must we?"

Perry and Jolly followed along the companion-ways and into a hatch where the officers' communal washrooms were. They looked a little more comfortable looking than those of the rest of the crew, as was to be expected.

"These are for the officers, but the captain's quarters have to be done, too," said Doherty. "Obviously, we'll see if we can do the captain's first, but before we set off, I would like you to look at the tiling on the floor and in the cubicles."

Perry looked at the white tiles, while Jolly allowed the chief steward to open the cubicle door for him to peer at the toilet basin. Everything appeared sparkling clean, then he saw the bolts that joined the stem of the lavatory to the floor. They had gone rusty, and grime had settled. Grime was also along the joins of the tiled floor and it was then he realised why they had brought old toothbrushes along.

Doherty turned to them. "I want you two lads to get down on your hands and knees and scrub right into those little crevices and clear all away. Understand, lads?" He waited for them to reply.

"Yes, Chief Steward," they replied with false vigour.

"That's the spirit, boys." Quartermaster Middleton winked at them, knowing they were trying to sound enthusiastic. "You're learning."

"We'll start you off in the captain's quarters then, lads," said Doherty with a smile. "I'll just get the captain's clearance."

He led them along another companionway to where these particular quarters were, and knocked upon a door. There came a muffled reply to enter, and in went the chief steward, closing the door behind him, leaving Middleton and his men to wait.

After a few moments, he emerged with a smile and said. "Send the men in, Quartermaster, the captain will see them. We can return to our duties." It was a subtle way of informing Middleton that he wouldn't be needed anymore.

The quartermaster stood back and held his hand towards the captain's door, smiling at the two seamen, who went forward nervously holding their mops, buckets with detergents and a collection of used toothbrushes.

"Don't let me down now, boys," whispered Middleton as they moved forward into the unexplored territory of the captain's quarters.

Inside, Captain McIntosh stood by his desk gathering papers and maps, with Commander Chudleigh standing beside him. He looked up as Perry and Jolly entered the room. "So, you're the luckless chaps that have landed this plum of annoying chores?"

"Yes, sir," they replied, timidly putting down their utensils, standing to attention and saluting.

"Very good. Don't worry, I don't bite unless I have to." His Scottish accent had a soothing effect on them. "It's through that hatch there. I'll leave you to it."

"Thank you, sir," they answered and went into the bathroom to commence with the job at hand.

Jolly lingered inside the entrance of the bathroom door. He was about to close it, but as usual, his curiosity got the better of him and he paused to get a quick look at the new captain. In doing so, he overheard the officers' chatter.

The captain grinned at Chudleigh and asked. "Either of those seamen been in trouble before, Number One?"

"No, Captain. Not to my knowledge, anyway."

"So they're just a couple of unfortunates in the wrong place at the wrong time." McIntosh smiled, shaking his head in amusement.

"I'm afraid so, Captain." Chudleigh raised an eyebrow in response to the captain's amusement.

"Happens to us all, one way or another. We'll go up to the bridge and see her out, shall we, Number One?"

"Yes, sir. So it's Foulness off the Essex coast now?"

"That's so," replied McIntosh, as though he found the new orders hard to believe. "It's something to do with this meteor that landed in Horsell Common near Woking."

"What? That thing rumoured to be from Mars?" laughed Chudleigh.

"That very thing indeed, and it's more than a meteor."

"What do you mean, Captain?"

"We'll it's something artificially crafted, and another has landed and more are on the way."

"How do we know?"

"Astronomers have been monitoring Mars and know things have happened there. Also, something emerged from the container that landed on the Common."

"Good God! This is amazing."

"Yes, there are some in the government that can't understand how panic hasn't started among the populace yet, but they fear something might happen due to an incident that was reported just before I came aboard."

"What was that, Captain?"

"There's been a report of a heat-ray weapon, and it's caused fatalities."

The captain moved to the hatchway and opened the cabin door, allowing Chudleigh to leave first. "Once we've put to sea, I'll inform the rest of the officers of the events unfolding as we speak."

The door slammed and Jolly gingerly shut the bathroom hatch he'd left ajar. He had heard the entire conversation.

"Bloody hell! Did you hear all that?" he said, as he got down on his hands and knees to scrub the grime within the tiles.

"Hear what? Ain't you got us into enough bloody trouble?" cursed Perry.

"No, this is it, mate. We're going to Foulness, off the Essex coast. It's something to do with that thing that fell from the sky in Woking. I read it in the newspaper Jennings brought aboard yesterday. 'Message Received from Mars' it read."

"What, the meteorite?"

"Yeah."

"Meteorites hit the earth every day. This one is tiny, compared to some that fall." Perry had been drinking in an inn the previous evening, listening to a learned gentleman who seemed knowledgeable on such matters.

"Oh 'ark at me. Mister Brains oozing out of me bleeding ear holes all of a sudden. What fell in Woking ain't no blooming meteorite. The captain said it was artificial."

"Yeah, that means unimportant," added Perry.

"Don't be an arse. It means it was made, unnatural—not created by nature. Like this ship."

"Why are we going to Foulness if the thing landed in Woking?"

"Perhaps we're going down-river? No, that can't be right. The captain said Foulness. He also said it had a heat-ray."

"That's near to my place," said Perry. "I'm from Leigh-on-Sea." The word 'heat-ray' didn't mean much to him. He thought it meant the meteor's fiery wake.

"Well, it should be nice for you, but all this is not good. Something else has happened, which has obviously prompted the powers that be to send the captain and us on our merry way to Foulness."

"How can you say something else has happened? Christ, Jolly! You're the biggest rumour-monger on board. We ain't even left yet and you've got me chewing me nails to me blooming elbows. Shut up and give your arse a chance, will you? Come on, let's get on with this or Middleton will be breathing down our necks." He began to scrub earnestly and, to his companion's credit, Jolly did too. But the topic did not end.

"You ain't one for taking notice of the news and all, are you?"

Jolly made the comment, knowing Perry didn't want to pursue the matter.

"You're not going to throw a sprat to catch a mackerel," answered Perry, aware of what Jolly was trying to do.

"Oh come on, Perry, it's a bloody exciting subject. Things like this don't happen every day. We could be on the brink of some fantastic historical event."

"For Christ's sake, it's just a bloody meteorite that landed on a common in Surrey. Wow! Yeah, all right, it's a rummy thing to have happened, but meteors have landed on this planet before. They land all the time, from what this upper-crust bloke was saying in the pub yesterday."

"That's right, Perry, some toff gives you the spill and you're all ear holes for it, ain't you? Well, the captain's a better toff with up-to-the-minute information. He's probably had telegrams sent from Parliament. That's why he got straight on board and said we're to go on a new course. It's also why he was able to tell Commander Chudleigh that the thing isn't natural, but artificial. Something created by beings from outer space, because something inside came out."

Perry frowned.

"He never said that."

"The captain said more are coming and astronomers have been monitoring Mars."

"Well how the bleeding hell can they monitor Mars?"

"With telescopes, you ignorant git," cussed Jolly. "Bloody hell, you're hard work."

For a long time, the two were locked in debate and speculation as they worked on long after the ironclad embarked upon its voyage. Often Perry would stop and ask Jolly if he was trying to tease him in some way, knowing he might be naïve and easy to get going, but no. Jolly was almost imploring and despondent in his efforts to try and convince Perry that he was right. They knew something many of the crew did not.

Eventually, the captain's door opened and both men fell silent in anticipation. They had worked hard cleaning the bathroom until it was immaculate, but then cleanliness was in the eye of the beholder and in the Royal Navy, the arbiters, were extremely particular. Chief Steward Doherty entered and a smile creased his usually emotionless face.

"Well, I must say that you lads appear to have done a fine job. A very fine effort indeed," he admitted as he looked around inspecting places here and there. Satisfied, he looked back at them. "Let's go back to the other washroom then. I think we can leave here now."

"Yes, Chief Steward," they replied, gathering their things and following Doherty out of the captain's quarters. He led them back along the companionway to the first bathroom they visited, stopping and smiling before the hatchway. They entered and set to work right away, wanting to get the job completed before any of the officers came in and messed up their work. This, however, was wishful thinking, because the washrooms were communal and there was regular traffic in the form of officers. None appeared to take notice of Perry and Jolly as they went about their business. Two of them spoke openly to each other about the strange meteorite that had landed in Horsell Common, wondering how such an event could provoke as much concern as it had. Neither seemed to elaborate on newspaper reports of life inside an artificial container. These were lower ranking officers who had only guessed at what the captain's briefing was in regard to and, when they left, Jolly couldn't help but comment.

"See, now do you believe me?"

Perry frowned. "They seem to think it's a meteorite still."

"That's because they weren't at the captain's briefing. They're living on rumours. We know more, because we overheard the captain."

"You mean you did," reaffirmed Perry as he pressed on with the cleaning.

Mister Stanley's Return to London

Albert Stanley was a meticulous man. He liked to go about things in the most appropriate manner and thus his important charge from the War Office instructing him to catch a train to Winchester was received with great resolve and gratitude. His original suspicion was that it had something to do with the meteorite at Horsell Common, near Woking.

That he, of all people, should be chosen for such an undertaking was surprising, but also encouraging to a person with his ambition.

The strange meteorite had caused such a fuss in the War Office and yet, when he'd passed through Woking train station en route to Winchester, there had seemed nothing untoward about the sleepy, suburban town. Perhaps a few more people walking along the platform than one would have expected, but then again it was a beautiful summer day and people were apt to do such things on fine days.

His task in Winchester was complete and he looked out the train window nonchalantly as it sped back to London—the meadows and hedge-rows swishing across his unimpressionable vision as the evening progressed. Only when entering a tunnel did he allow his vision to become stimulated, and that was by his reflection staring back. He noted the droopy, ginger moustache plastered across the fat, white head with the bulbous red nose; the long red strands from the left side were greased and combed across the pink expanse of his sweating, bald head. He was not the most confident-looking man, and was nervous around the female sex. Quickly dismissing such failings, he looked directly into his own reflected eyes and thought, *"Well, well, you've done well, Mr Stanley. Very well indeed."*

He always imagined there was another him, lavishing praise upon himself, while in the background, his proud old mother looked on with an appropriate smile. He saw her little entourage of tea-and-cake friends nodding their heads approvingly, and she would say, "He works for the government, you know."

"Who would have thought that a man of your humble background would be chosen for such an important task?" enquired his ego-massaging reflection.

The countryside swept his reflection away on a tide of trees, meadows and hedgerows, and he was forced to sit back and ponder.

He had done his duty and rendezvoused with Captain McIntosh before the man had left for his ship, *HMS Thunder Child*. What was contained in the despatch case was beyond him, but he had sent the telegram back to the War Office informing them the duty was accomplished, before boarding the train back to London.

His self-indulgence was suddenly interrupted as the train slowed to a halt just short of Woking station. It was only at that moment that he noticed the rest of the commuters were decidedly uneasy. Then a distant boom, like a piece of field artillery going off, brought home the recognition that he'd heard the sound before and hadn't heeded it while lost in his fantasising excess.

"What on earth is going on?" asked one bemused gentleman.

Before anyone could answer, a clamour of human screams was heard from further along the track as though it was drawing closer to the stationary train—an approaching wave of panic.

Albert stood up, along with the rest of the people in the carriage. "Good Lord, what is that awful racket?" he demanded, fearfully.

Then arose a series of explosions, and the human pandemonium intensified. The train jolted into motion and everyone in the carriage swayed to the movement, including Albert as his heart thumped excitedly. Adrenaline pulsed through his body as he looked around in panic with the rest of the passengers.

"We're going backwards," a woman's voice called out in panic.

The furious roar, and erupting balls of flame smashing through the carriage windows, were the last vision Albert recollected before the blackness took him. Somewhere in the darkness was the cacophony of screaming people, which drifted into the oblivion. Briefly, the memory was erased. For how long, he couldn't say, but he remembered being aware of travelling along a red spiral, shortly before coming out of the void and regaining consciousness.

It was night; all around him were scattered fires in the smoke-filled carriage. He raised himself, coughing and spluttering, his body aching and his clothes covered in dust, torn and singed. Gingerly, he raised himself from the slopping carriage floor, feeling the night breeze ruffling the hair hanging down his left side. The roof of the train was gone, and he could see the stars, and smell the burning fires—their crackling embers wickedly serenading the summer night. Hurting, still slightly incoherent, he managed to clamber through the twisted doorway to stand outside among the burning debris. Bodies were littered along the railway line— blackened, burning corpses that filled the air with the acrid smell of burning flesh. Among the scattered corpses, smoking craters littered the railway embankment, from which emitted a spent black smoke. On inhaling, his lungs were violently stung, even though it was thinly dispersed. He retched, lowered himself to the shingle in an attempt to be away from the hovering fumes. The stinging gradually subsided, but his lungs were sore as though something inside his chest was clawing to get out. Fumbling inside his pocket, he pulled out his handkerchief and quickly put it over his mouth, preferring to breathe through the material. After allowing a few minutes to get over the intense trauma that had wracked his chest, he surveyed his surroundings in more detail. It was a vision of hell, and he was the only thing that moved amid the scene of tribulation. The charred bodies disturbed him with their flayed postures. It was evident they had been writhing in agony as their bodies were scorched. All had died kicking and thrashing—frozen in their final, agonised moments; scorched effigies, with blackened, twisted fingers pointing to the heavens accusingly—as though created by some demonic sculptor hysterically giggling in eternity at the arrogant little insects scattered before it.

Albert jumped at the sound of shingle spilling from the embankment and clutched his chest, thinking his heart might give up on him. It was a railway worker—a lean, middle-aged man with thick, matted hair who looked every bit as dishevelled as Albert himself. He was also holding a blackened handkerchief over his mouth. Descending, he made his way towards Albert, who began to calm at the sight of another human being.

"Take this," said the railwayman. He had a northern accent.

Albert complied and took some torn rag. It was damp and wrapped around a lump of coal. "What is it?" he asked.

"Put it to thee mouth, man. Breathe through it."

"What does it do?" Albert put the thing to his mouth.

"I used to work in mines. It's an old trick that me grandfather spoke of. I can't say as it works like, but there was loads of coal spilt by the engine and when I fell, I put it to my mouth."

"What happened here? I've only just got out of the carriage. The last thing I can remember is the train reversing and the fire coming through the windows. I heard guns going off…"

"The guns were ours, I think," cut in the engine man. "They had been firing at the things before everywhere was overrun by them. I think they came from the Common."

"What things?" Albert frowned. "Not the meteorites."

"I only saw one, but I think there might have been another, because I could hear it further off."

"What things?" Albert repeated.

"It was a giant machine on three legs. The top was like some sort of container cabin, standing high, towering over everything. There were sparks hitting the thing where bullets bounced off it. It fired at the train as we reversed. People scrambled out of the wreckage and were blasted by a heat-ray. God, the screams! It were awful and then came the black smoke and I could see them grabbing their throats and choking. I lay amid the scattered coal and steaming water. I realised it were some sort of gas and I remembered my grandfather telling of wet rags wrapped in coal. I buried my bloody head in the stuff while all around I could hear the flash of the heat gun and the choking. It were ages before I dared to raise my head and look. The thing had gone and everyone were dead."

"How long ago was this?"

"God knows. I got up and have been along the entire length of the train and found no living soul, save yourself."

"I was knocked unconscious when the train first crashed."

"Aye, and that's what saved you, no doubt. Inside the carriage, you were missed by the…" he lingered, not knowing what to call the tripod.

"The thing," added Albert obligingly.

"Yes and, no doubt, being inside protected you from the black smoke, too."

"I got a breath full when I got out."

"Yeah, but most 'as scattered now."

"There seems to be no emergency services. I would have thought rescue workers might be here by now. How far away is Woking station?" asked Albert.

"It's there," the man pointed eastwards along the track to a blaze where flames were devouring a building. There were more fires in the town. "That's Woking."

From beyond in the distance came the sound of a further artillery barrage as lights flickered on the northeast horizon. Both watched the flickers beyond the inferno that was Woking town.

"Whatever these things are, they're trying to get towards London," said Albert as he moved a few paces forward.

"Well, somewhere along the road, they're going to come up against the entire bloody army. The things are good, but not that good, surely."

"There are more meteors coming," added Albert. "Lots more."

As though on cue, a meteorite flashed across the star-filled sky like a shooting star blazing a trail downwards towards the earth.

"How bloody many more?" asked the engineman.

"God knows. They come from Mars. We're being invaded by aliens from Mars." He looked up to the sky in wonder and muttered. "Why are they sending me on errands to the men of our navy? What use is our vast navy against this lot?"

"Beats me," said the bemused engineman. "They cut out the sea journey and literally just drop in."

Albert looked at the man nervously, then added. "The emergency services. Fire brigade, ambulances and police are gone too, aren't they?"

The dishevelled engine driver looked at him and nodded his agreement. He looked towards London. "Do you have people in the City?"

"My mother is in Stoke Newington."

"What will you do?"

"I don't think I'll be able to do anything." He found his reason kicking in and his ability to become cold and hard during a crisis was falling into order. "London will not be a place to go to, but one that will be rapidly deserted. I'm heading south. The War Office was expecting this. I'm sure of that. Now I know why I was sent on this errand. I'm expendable I suppose and they'll be needed for more serious tasks."

"Are you saying they knew this was going to happen?" asked the engineman.

"They knew things were becoming uneasy when I was sent a telegram at Winchester. It said that visitors were killed at the drop site when something emerged from the rock."

Together, Albert and the engine driver watched the flashing lights and listened to the sound of the guns on the distant horizon. A short time ago, he had been travelling through the Surrey countryside languishing beneath a beautiful summer twilight. Suddenly, both men were standing in hell on earth, as the new deranged surroundings burned. A new apocalyptic landscape that breathed fire, smoke and death.

"We'll need to inform the army about your makeshift mask. It might prove useful," said Albert.

"I can't say as for sure," added the engine worker.

"No, but there'll be no harm in trying. I'm going south. If I come across any telegraph office, I'll inform them to despatch this advice."

"Should we not wait here for someone to come?"

Mister Stanley ran his hand over his sweating head and felt irritation at the thin strands of hair hanging on his left shoulder—the same pathetic wisps he had combed over his head in a futile attempt to hide his baldness. "My dear fellow, no one is coming. This is the shape of things to come. I'm not sure what to do, but I'm certain going to London wouldn't be constructive. The only worthwhile thing I can think of doing is informing people of your idea about confronting the black gas. It might work, it might not, but if everyone does their one little thing, it can be millions of practical steps in the right direction."

"Well, a crisis certainly brings out the best in you, Mister...er..."

"Stanley," replied Albert.

"Well, it does indeed, Mister Stanley. I don't know what to do."

"You're married, aren't you, sir?"

"Yes, Mister Stanley. I am."

"Not in London."

"No, thankfully, Mister Stanley."

"Then go to them now, man. Go to them."

"I don't think the rail board will be too impressed with me leaving the scene of carnage and all. I'll get sacked."

"Good God, man." Albert stopped himself from getting angry. He thought the wretched man before him. "Now look, my good man. I'm from the government. The War Office, and I carry authoritative powers." He rummaged through his jacket and produced papers of legitimacy, plus a notebook and pen. "What is your name, sir?" he enquired.

"Reginald Fredrick Simmerson," replied the engineman. He looked through the papers that had been given to him while Albert Stanley wrote a note firmly ordering the rail worker to return home and look for his wife.

"There, you've been ordered by the government and I might tell you, Mister Simmerson, it is a custodial offence to disobey."

The engine driver smiled nervously. "Thank you, Mister Stanley. Much obliged to you."

The world had gone mad and some people couldn't grasp it. Fortunately, Albert Stanley could. He stood amid carnage and destruction, wishing for a pair of scissors to cut off the last, stupid vestiges of his silly old shortcomings. The blithering strands of silly hair hanging down the left side of his head.

CHAPTER 2
THE CAPTAIN'S BRIEFING

Captain McIntosh watched *Thunder Child* steam out of the harbour towards the approaching dusk and into the English Channel, where they set a course to follow the coast eastward. He watched the surf erupt over the descending bow, drenching the deck's capstans and anchor chains with slithering, white foam that rushed out through hawse pipes and spilled over the side as the forecastle lifted again. It was a pleasing sight, and normally he would have liked to stay on the bridge to watch the coastal defence vessel's progress. But the need to debrief his senior officers was paramount. For this reason, he became anxious to get on with things, and left the bridge early.

"Very good, Lieutenant Faulbs, take over. I'll send someone to relieve you shortly and fill you in, once I've informed the others of what's going on."

"Thank you, Captain." The lieutenant assumed his position, while others watched and wondered what the rush was about, sensing there was some urgent purpose in the departing captain's manner.

Quickly, he made his way aft, along the super-structure and down the ladder to the top of the rear turret, then nimbly down another ladder on the side of the revolving armour at the back by the hatch—beyond which, the aft gun crew would be. It was as though he knew the ship inside out—how or why, he couldn't say. Walking to the next stair-way that descended from the main deck to the quarterdeck, he paused, thinking the vessel was most odd indeed. Almost like a Devastation class in looks, but too small. If she had one funnel, then she might be a Cyclops class, though he had to admit—her layout was more like that of a miniature *HMS Devastation*—a ship he'd once visited when he was in Malta over ten years ago as a young officer.

He looked to port, where the Southern English coast was green and glorious in the blue June sky. It was then that the ominous and bizarre notion struck him. Britons always expected to use ships to defend themselves from foreign aggressors, but this time, they were already deep within the heartland of their country. The Martians had gone straight for the jugular. No battling across the sea—fighting a path through the world's biggest navy. Instead, they had fallen from the sky and cut out all the middle-men. He shook his head as he went into the hatch behind the stairway and again went downwards to the main deck, making his way aft.

Arriving at the wardroom, he was pleasantly surprised by the interior. Only the three portholes looked odd within the wood panelling, which gave the room a more traditional appeal. His officers were standing behind chairs that went along the conference table. In an effort to put his officers at ease, he smiled as he closed the door.

"Please be seated, gentlemen." He walked to his chair at the head of the table as everyone sat down. On the wall behind him was a framed black and white photo of *Thunder Child*.

"Well, I'll get down to the issue right away. This thing that's landed in Horsell Common, near Woking—the meteorite that fell from the sky. I'm sure you have all read about it."

There came a murmur of agreement from those assembled. All had, indeed, heard of the phenomenon.

"Well, things have begun to happen which have caused great concern and anxiety. I can confirm that the container is something artificial. In this,

I mean it was created by an extra-terrestrial intelligence and is believed to have come from Mars. There is a life form inside the container, which we now know is hostile. There are reports of another landing, too. This has only just been confirmed, as has an account of some fatalities among some sightseers who approached the Horsell Common container. This news I received by telegram about half-an-hour before coming aboard. So, as we speak, more incidents may be occurring. London has suddenly been gripped by panic, and troops have been sent to cordon off the area."

Chudleigh asked the first question. "Will we be informed of events along the way, sir?"

"Yes," confirmed the captain. "Signalmen are stationed to receive information from the shore-line stations all along the coast in order for us to keep abreast of the situation. Besides our own navy, foreign ships from Europe will be coming close to our shores as well. We will rendezvous with vessels from France and Germany along the way. This is at the request of the British Government. Our destination is Foulness, at the mouth of the Thames estuary. There is concern that the country will soon be in the grip of mass hysteria and people might start evacuating the City. Many will want to leave the country. This can cause a tremendous refugee problem, and we are to prepare for an emergency."

The captain stopped and, for a moment, there was stunned silence as the unbelievable information was digested by his staff. Then came the first question:

"Do you think it will come to mass evacuation, Captain?"

"Personally, no, but this is a precautionary measure only. We don't know what we're up against, hence this foresight activity. Obviously, there are more serious aspects to these manoeuvres, which is why foreign navies are participating."

Chudleigh cleared his throat as all heads turned to him. "Have you only been communicated with by telegram, sir?"

"No, this morning a man from the War Office came to see me, but events had overtaken him en route. For instance, the fatalities from the heat-ray were as much a surprise to him as they were to me."

"Heat-ray!" they exclaimed in shock.

The captain sighed. "Yes, they were killed by a blast from a heat-ray. This is the event which caused the panic. Evidently, until then, people weren't taking much notice of it at all. The locals from Woking and Ottershaw were walking over the heath to look at what was going on. Some astronomers turned up and began digging around the container while the crowds watched. Things become a little surreal after that. There are reports of the container lid unscrewing and weird alien creatures crawling out and falling into the pit. It caused something of a panic and the crowd dispersed to a safe distance to make out what was happening. After a while, a group of the excavators or astronomers returned under a white flag of truce. They were killed by some form of heat-ray and the surrounding area was scorched as well. The rest of the onlookers fled. Now, however, there appears to be a strong sense of urgency. Even abroad, concern is growing."

"Are all signal stations on standby then, sir?"

"Yes, the coastline is a hive of activity and all stations are in direct contact with London. We will get up-to-the-minute information when we pass them, and they're constantly transmitting to all naval vessels. We'll also be putting some of our own signalmen aboard the French vessel *FS Courbet*, the largest central battery ship ever built. They will liaise with our allies so that signal information is readily available to them. The same will go for the *Konig Wilhelm*. The Germans have just re-done her boilers and taken her sail rigs down. She is now a re-commissioned armoured cruiser with much improved armaments. So, gentlemen, besides the vast array of ships from our own force, we will have the combined might of France and Germany with us, plus there are Spanish, Italian and American ships on course, too."

"What do we tell the rest of the crew, sir?"

"For the moment, nothing. It's probable this will be the biggest storm in a teacup that has ever happened and I, for one, will welcome the embarrassment of being red-faced among our allies when the blooming affair is over." The captain looked down at his hands resting on the table and took a deep breath. "It seems however, that every time I get information, something more bizarre has happened."

A knock sounded at the door and the guard entered instantly. "Captain, sorry to interrupt, but Lieutenant Faulbs says you're needed on the bridge with the utmost urgency."

The captain stood. "Tell him I'm on my way. Number One, accompany me please."

"Yes, sir," replied Chudleigh.

Everyone stood, wanting to know more—there had to be further information. They were also curious as to what Lieutenant Faulbs was so excited about. Quickly, the captain, accompanied by Chudleigh, walked along the companionways grim-faced and bracing himself for the next bit of unbelievable news. As he entered the bridge, all eyes were turned to him, almost imploring. *What on earth was going on?* Faulbs handed him a note. It simply read:

20.17 am Fierce fighting against alien tripods around Woking. Tripod weapons are heat-rays and jets of black steam. Defences breached. Local population in panic. Government has proclaimed Woking a disaster area. Measures being undertaken to cope with refugees vacating area.

"This signal is being constantly transmitted, sir," said Lieutenant Faulbs.

Captain McIntosh was stunned, but his mind began to move ahead. They still had the French and German vessels to meet beyond Dover. They would proceed with this and go on to Foulness.

"The signal station has just gone out of view, sir, but the next one will be coming about in fifteen minutes."

"Very good, Lieutenant, I'll take the bridge. Where's the signalman?"

"Back on the port semaphore, Captain."

"Don't let anyone else talk with him for the moment. We don't want this around the ship yet."

"Yes, Captain," replied Faulbs.

"I would like you to go outside with the signalman and allow Commander Chudleigh to enlighten you."

Again, Faulbs replied. "Yes, Captain." He walked out the hatchway.

"I presume the signalman will have to know the full story," checked Chudleigh.

"Yes, or he'll start speculating," replied Captain McIntosh as he called down the voice pipe to give the helmsman direction adjustments. "Two points starboard, then full ahead."

He looked out through the window where Chudleigh had followed the lieutenant outside. As the young officer was informed of the strange and terrible matters at hand, his face was contorted in disbelief, even though much was known because of the messages. It was probably the authenticity Chudleigh brought which amazed Faulbs.

Unable to see their facial expressions, Captain McIntosh went out onto the open bridge with them.

"As ludicrous as it sounds, Faulbs, it's true."

He closed the hatch door and watched the bow slice into the sea, showering the halyard and fore turret with an onslaught of fierce, white drizzle. "It's happening, and now. I thought the newspapers were vague and nothing much had been reported apart from a strange belief the meteor wasn't natural."

"So it is accepted that there are creatures? Hostile, intelligent creatures invading us?" Faulbs wanted it confirmed once more.

The captain nodded, then added. "I can't believe I'm telling you this, but yes. Right now as we speak, they must be going through Surrey and heading for the southwest outskirts of London."

"Why are we going to Foulness if the trouble started in Woking, sir?"

"We think it's likely there the refugees will be fleeing. If these things enter from a westerly direction, those fleeing will probably go east. They might want to leave the country."

"Do you expect it to come to that?" asked Faulbs.

"I didn't at first. Even during the briefing. But since receiving your message, I'm not sure. It's as I've already said. It would be wonderfully silly if it was all a storm in a teacup, but every time we get more information, it seems to be more fantastic. Fearfully so."

Chudleigh shook his head in disbelief and began to think of the term 'tripod'. "Why are these Martians being referred to as tripods? I keep visualising some three-legged spiderlike beings."

"None of the population, except for those in and around Woking, know what the aliens look like," added the captain. "Though I must confess— the word 'tripod' conjures up an image like yours, Number One."

"What are they then? Three-legged men? How many could fit into one of those canister things?"

Chudleigh was perplexed and looked into the window. The bridge was gloomy and, out of the rear shutters across the superstructure, the sun began to sink below the horizon. The spreading wake left the aft deck, scattering white foam from port and star-board stern while above, seagulls hovered in front of the declining orange ball.

Faulbs was equally lost. "Not many, sir. So how could the Armed Forces surrounding them have been defeated?"

The captain retained his unruffled demeanour. "They would be technologically more advanced than us, but even then, I would have thought supe-riority of numbers and our own technology might have sufficed for the one canister. The papers main-tained it was long, but not big enough to carry an army."

"It has to be the weapons," suggested Chudleigh. "The heat-rays and black steam. If they are able to displace it over wide areas quickly, they might be able to sterilise an area before moving forward."

"Yes, then with just a few of them, they might be able to mop up with heat-rays," agreed Faulbs.

"And now there are more canisters with new tri-pod troops. This might be the tip of the iceberg."

They tried again to visualise how these creatures must look, as an eerie sensation clawed in the pit of each man's stomach. Despite it being fantastic, none disbelieved the true nature of what was happening. The papers had reported the strange meteorite that had fallen near Woking and had established it was artificial in origin before *Thunder Child* had disembarked. All believed in the authenticity of the reports but may have been inclined to think things were being hyped up. None realised how unimportant people viewed the affair. Now, with the benefit of hindsight, they could see the matter had been played down enormously.

"The next signal station is coming up, sir," announced the signalman, who had come through the bridge to inform the captain. The semaphore was to the rear of the bridge on the superstructure.

"You had better take the bridge," said Chudleigh to Faulbs. "I think we'll want to be out here with the signalman."

"Yes, sir."

The reply followed as they went back through the hatch.

The signalman was already encrypting the message on a notepad and quickly tore off a sheet for the captain. He read it aloud.

"Maybury Hill destroyed. More tripods being assembled from other fallen canisters. Army annihilated. Death toll mounts."

"Good God," said Chudleigh. "There must be something we can do."

"Is he repeating the same message?" asked Captain McIntosh calmly as his fingers stroked his chin.

"Yes, sir."

"I want you to send him a message. Ask them if they know what these aliens actually look like."

The signalman immediately began to flash *Thunder Child*'s message, and then spoke excitedly. "They're replying, sir." He began eagerly scribbling, then passed the note on.

Once again, the captain read the message aloud for Chudleigh. "Tripods are armoured encasements that stand one hundred feet plus. Inside each is the protected Martian. They fire heat-rays and jets of black smoke. They are guarding another meteor, presumed to be harbouring more Martians. Further meteors are falling. All approaches towards tripods are dealt with severely."

"Any further information?" asked Chudleigh.

"No, sir. He's repeating the original message and then the answer to the captain's question."

"Ask when additional information is expected," ordered the captain, to which the signalman swiftly responded. Concern etched on his face as he handed the next message to the captain.

"Lines of communication down. Despatch riders sent. Will have to see if next station is operative," the captain said, then added. "Their telegraph lines must run close by the Woking area, which means this section of coastline is now cut off."

"It's getting worse by the minute, sir."

"Yes, but we must still progress with our mission. I'm almost glad we're out here and not on land," admitted the captain. He looked to the signalman. "Thank them and wish them luck."

"Yes, Captain."

Mister Stanley Visits the Lighthouse

"Away from the world and all its stress, that's how I looks at it, lad. Anyone who tells you it's a strain is not being as honest as he might be."

The principal keeper didn't like to call a person a liar, even if he wasn't talking about anyone in particular. He rubbed his long, grey sideburns and felt uncomfortable at the thought of speaking harshly of an imaginary someone. "I'm not saying as I've heard other lighthouse folk say as much, mind."

He went to the doorway beyond, which was the dingy staircase that hugged the inner funnelled wall of the lighthouse tower. Briefly, he stopped to look at the cracked and peeling off-white gloss of the doorframe.

"I reckon I agrees with you there, sir," agreed the supernumerary assistant keeper. SAK Edward Salmon, the young apprentice, was an enthusiastic lad, who had gained the principal keeper's favour. "I feel settled already. Nothing can touch us out here. We're away from the world and all its problems." He looked to the doorjambs. "I'll rub it down and give it a recoat."

The principal keeper grinned. "You'll make good, young Salmon. You've got the makings of a keeper. I can tell." The old man of the tower light nodded, then continued up the staircase, with Salmon in pursuit. "You've got your foot in the door as SAK and now it's a year's probation I believe."

"That's right. I'm eight months into the probation now and this is my fourth duty. Two land lights and one rock and now, this tower."

The principal stopped then looked back, smiling. "Well you're getting your jargon right, lad. So, four months to go and then the S for supernumerary is dropped and the assistant keeper bit is all that's left." He had an amused smile, as though he thought the word supernumerary was full of pomp and unnecessary. They continued up towards the lantern and went out onto the gallery, where the seagulls were more numerous and noisy than usual—a fact they neglected to note, for they were hit by the sight of something even more unusual.

The sea was full of vessels, almost like a vast regatta of shipping. There was every type of ship, boat, yacht and tug one could imagine. Everything was heading eastwards.

The principal stood stiffly and SAK Salmon could tell the sight was perplexing, even with his limited experience. Neither had seen the sea-lanes containing so much traffic, ever.

"My, there's an awful lot of shipping out there today." The principal frowned and shook his head. "This is extremely strange."

"I were thinking that, too," agreed young Salmon. "It don't seem natural to me."

"No, lad. It doesn't. You get a feel when something's wrong, and this lays none too good in my reckoning."

"There's German and French battleships out there…"

"I know, lad, and what's strange, they're alongside our dreadnoughts, look. They seem perfectly at ease with one another. I would have said it was an exercise, but then, there wouldn't be all the smaller merchant vessels and yachts, too."

Salmon took off his cap and scratched his ginger mop. "It is very strange, indeed. What do you think is going on?"

The principal leaned over the gallery rails and frowned. "There's a Royal Navy vessel coming to the tower, lad. I'll get below. I'll wake Walsh from his beauty sleep, too. I think he might be needed." He disappeared, leaving Salmon to watch the vessel's approach. It was an old Cyclops class coastal defence ship. It dropped anchor a short distance off, and a small boat was despatched with a team of signalmen on board. He watched with interest as the boat drew closer to the tower light. His curiosity was aroused, but there was nothing he could do to find out what the Royal Navy men wanted. He waited patiently for the principal's return while the approaching boat went from view beneath the tower light's gantry.

The seagulls' squawking died as he went back into the lantern room and closed the door. He had only realised their presence when their sound was removed. There had been far too many other things of interest to occupy his thoughts. Through the glass, he again became transfixed by the flow of shipping. It was colossal, and had appeared from nowhere in a short space of time.

"What on earth could cause such a thing?" he muttered to himself. He thought of an earthquake. There had been one in Essex in 1886, but then the tremors would have been felt along the south coast. No! Maybe not and the sea traffic was cruising east. It would pass Dover and go north to Essex. He whispered. "Earthquakes can return and be more vigorous than the first time." It had to be bad with such an array of vessels, including foreign ships, too. That had to be it. Essex had another and more violent earthquake. It was the only explanation—a geological disaster.

He heard voices coming up the staircase, one belonging to the principal keeper, but the other was unfamiliar. No doubt someone from the coastal defence vessel. He strained to listen to the approaching voices.

"Well, we shall do our utmost to accommodate the navy men, but how they'll recognise *Thunder Child* out there is beyond me, Mister Stanley. There's more vessels out there than I've ever seen."

Salmon took a step back as the keeper rounded the final part of the stairwell, followed by a small bald man. He looked like an authoritative person, but with his shirtsleeves rolled up and his suit jacket apparently discarded, he had that rough-around-the-edge aspect—the look of a man who led and mucked in at the same time. Two Royal Navy signalmen followed, carrying equipment Salmon thought might be for communicating with the shipping.

"The navy lads will know *Thunder Child*," stated Mister Stanley as he stepped aside, allowing the signalmen to access the balcony. "Right after I received the telegram from London, the lines went dead. They need to get the ship to go to Maldon in Essex."

"Along the River Blackwater. I knows the place," said the keeper, still perplexed. "What's happening, Mister Stanley? We don't get much news out here, but out there…" He nodded towards the open sea, where the mass of shipping was moving eastwards. "Well, out there, things seem awful strange."

"Indeed things are, sir. We're being invaded by Martians from out of space." There was a dry look on Mister Stanley's face, and Salmon thought he instantly recognised that dry middle-class British sense of humour.

The principal keeper stood there, not knowing how to react. He turned to Salmon, who had a grin on his face, and only then did he conclude Mister Stanley was politely but firmly telling him not to take too much of an interest in military and War Office affairs.

"Oh, begging your pardon and all that, Mister Stanley. We won't stand in your way if you 'as to be dealing with Martians from out of space and all that malarkey." He winked, allowing Mister Stanley to know that lighthouse men didn't go about showing too much interest in affairs that weren't of their concern.

Mister Stanley raised his eyebrow. He decided he received a small response and that it would be rather tedious to go through his adventures yet again. He bade his farewell and left the lighthouse men to the mercy of the signalmen who would, no doubt, let them know that Martians were on the rampage in Britain.

The principal keeper waited for him to get out of sight and then whispered to Salmon. "Very dry, these men of government authority."

"He certainly has got a very subtle way of telling us folk to mind our own business," agreed Salmon.

A warm smile settled on the keeper's face. "You could say that again, lad. That's what makes these men what they are." His face wore that look of sublime awe. "Pure breeding that is, boy. They know how to dance a sidestep when they don't want to tell you something"

"That's what makes this country of ours great," agreed Salmon.

The door to the balcony opened and one of the navy signalmen walked in. He was a cheery looking fellow who smiled politely.

"We'll not get in your way too much," said the Welsh sailor.

"That's all right, lad," said the principal keeper. "How many of you chaps are staying on the tower during this…" He grinned. "Martian lark?"

"There's a small landing party that will be with us. They're disembarking now. I saw them when I looked down from the balcony. They're armed and a few of them will be stationed up here and the others will stay at the bottom of the tower.

"That's to defend the door in case spacemen try to break in, aye?" added Salmon humorously.

"Well, you never know," replied the sailor as he passed and went down the stairs. He called back as he descended. "From what I've heard, they're so tall they could get in over the balcony."

The principal keeper chuckled. "Well bless my soul. They're all in on the act."

Salmon agreed. "Very highly trained in being evasive about things, aren't they?"

"Indeed they are, lad. Still, I suppose we can indulge them a bit."

CHAPTER 3

THE QUARTERMASTER RETURNS

"Well now!" The quartermaster's voice had caught them unaware. "What's all the banter then?"

Perry, confounded, looked to Jolly for a way out—blast the man, he had done it again! Shooting his mouth off without regard for who might be around, and Middleton had caught them chatting away like a couple of wet hens.

"We've just about finished in here, Quarter-master," said Jolly as he stood up.

Middleton's expression became severe. "I never asked you that, boy. Now gather your things and follow me."

They collected their cleaning gear, then dismally followed Middleton back to the stores. He made them put all the things away, while remaining silent. This was not a good sign. When finished, they stood to attention before him.

"Now," he whispered. "You, Jolly, were gossiping away like a bloody wet hen, and I want to know how you seem to be so enlightened and if at any time, I get a whiff of the dishonest John Bull—you're going to wish you were never bloody born, understand, lad?"

"Yes, Quartermaster," replied Jolly.

"Right, what do you know and what have you heard? No nonsense, I want how and where you got your information. Tell me the officers you heard saying such things in your presence." Middelton was determined to get everything and it was obvious Jolly wouldn't know how much the quartermaster knew. He reasoned the young guttersnipe would flit around facts here and there, but he would spot these manifestations and come down heavy on him straight away. It was all part of the game and he could play little urchins like Jolly and Perry all day long. It wouldn't take them long to fall in line. "You see, boys, it's not your fault if you overhear something you shouldn't. It's more the fact you allowed yourselves to get caught blabbering about it. First, I'll hear your side of the story, Jolly. Then Perry can give me his succulent little rendition of this wonderfully gripping yarn I'm about to hear." Middleton's flippant humour was returning.

Jolly took a deep breath and was about to begin, but Middleton stopped him dead in his tracks. "Whoa there, boy. My word, you're a very eager young chap, aren't you? First, I want Perry to go into the next room and shut the hatch. Then stand at the furthest wall with your fingers in your ears. Have you got that, young Perry?"

"Yes, Quartermaster." He made off straightaway and shut the hatchway door behind him.

"Well now, Jolly, I'm all lug holes for yours truly, and God help you if Perry's story ain't the same. You see, lad, I want the name of the careless officer who allowed you to overhear what sounded like classified information about these Martian things that have fallen."

"I never meant to overhear, Quartermaster. It was an accident, honest to God."

Middleton gave him a fatherly smile. "I'm sure you didn't, boy. But information, the likes of which you were talking about isn't fit for the rest of the crew to hear at the moment. And much of it sounded a little too fantastic for me to believe. Nonetheless, you can't go around rumour-mongering about this blooming meteorite thing that's fallen at Woking. That's what you were on about and now you're saying we're on missions because of Martian monsters killing folk with heat-rays. That's what I heard you say, lad, so don't deny it."

"I'm not trying to deny it, sir. I did hear that, it's true."

Middleton sniggered. "Come on, lad, surely you're not sucked in by all this."

"It's true, sir, honestly. I swear I accidentally overheard this being said."

"Well, give me the officer's name. The captain will be informed of the matter. We can't have this here sort of thing going on aboard ship. Now don't worry, lad, you won't be in trouble for this one. Officers should know when the likes of you are in the vicinity and take care of their idle toilet gossip."

"It's not quite like that, sir…"

"Nonsense, lad, tell me who you heard talking this drivel."

"The captain said it to Commander Chudleigh, sir."

Middleton grunted. He was spellbound, and cut to the quick. How could he sort out the careless officer by reporting the misdemeanour to the captain, when that very person made the mistake in the first place? The man was hardly likely to let himself off with a stern warning.

Jolly related the incident—about not closing the hatchway to the captain's bathroom properly. How on going back to shut the door, he overheard the conversation, also admitting that Perry didn't hear the discussion, only what had been told him afterwards. He told of the captain's words concerning the heat-ray and fatalities.

Bemused, Middleton went into the next room and allowed Perry to tell his version of events, which complied with Jolly's. When this was done, he became perplexed in front of his two subordinates. He believed them, though he hoped they might have misinterpreted the captain, but he had read enough in the newspaper, which had seemed to report the matter with less importance than it deserved.

"I've never heard anything so fantastic in all my life. Bloody heat-rays."

"Can we go now, Quartermaster?" asked Jolly, hoping he'd caught Middleton at a weak moment.

"No, the pair of you stay here and don't leave this place until I get back, understood?"

"Yes, Quartermaster," they complied.

Perry looked to Jolly, who was gritting his teeth and cursing the day he ever fell in with this fellow who found it agony to keep his mouth shut, even for a minute. The hatch door closed as the quartermaster left them, allowing Perry to lavishly discharge a scathing bombardment of colourful metaphors upon his companion.

As Middleton walked along the companionway, he could scarcely come to grips with what was going on and felt apprehensive at approaching the captain on the matter. He made his way onto the quarter-deck, bathed in the starlit night, to the central ladder way that led to the main deck where the short, stubby twelve-inch aft guns barely protruded from the revolving turret. All around, the sound of the sea was therapeutic; relaxing him somewhat, and making him feel more at ease about approaching Captain McIntosh.

He reasoned that Jolly and Perry should not be let loose with such knowledge—Jolly especially, the urchin couldn't be trusted to keep his mouth shut—and if the captain wanted to keep things quiet, something would have to be done with both lads. Progressing along the starboard freeboard, he stopped at the hatchway, which led into the pilot-house, where the helmsman was taking directions from the bridge.

"Is the captain giving directions personally?"

"No, Quartermaster, its Lieutenant Faulbs, but the captain is aloft."

"Good." He looked out through the starboard hatch's porthole back into the night and decided he was positive about pursuing the matter. Then with new determination, he climbed the conning tower ladder onto the superstructure, where two lifeboats hung on either side, gently swinging in the clear night air. The breeze and the sound of a tranquil sea soothed him and he passed the fore funnel in front of the bridge. Outside, by the hatchway, he saw the captain at the port semaphore with a signalman, who was communicating with an onshore station using a torch. It was a clear night and stars sparkled their radiance amid the gentle sound of the surf.

He felt somewhat irregular in his approach, but then he was sure the matter warranted immediate attention and, waiting for the lights to stop, the quartermaster allowed Captain McIntosh to complete communications with land. Commander Chudleigh stepped out of the hatch, wanting to know what the message said.

"What is it, Quartermaster?" asked the captain, deciding to deal with Middleton straight away.

"Got a bit of a problem, Captain, concerning the two sailors that cleaned your ablutions. They overheard yourself and Commander Chudleigh on a matter of heat-rays. Don't really want to send them back among the rest of the crew without your consent, Captain."

The delicacy of the situation was realised at once and the captain sighed despondently. "Yes, Quartermaster, this isn't good at all. Right, I want them up here away from the rest of the crew. Now what can they do to keep occupied?"

Middleton looked at the wooden deck panels and suggested. "How about a little wood stain and varnishing, Captain?"

"Very good, Quartermaster. See to it, will you?"

"At once, Captain." He turned and was about to make his way back.

"Quartermaster."

Middleton stopped. "Sorry, Captain, I didn't know there would be anything else." He had done the unthinkable and dismissed himself in front of the captain.

McIntosh smiled briefly. He felt he should let the quartermaster know more. He appeared to be a quick thinking man. "You've no doubt heard of the reports second-hand. I can confirm that we are in a grave situation where these Martians are concerned."

"Martians, Captain? You mean this meteorite business?"

"You're a quartermaster. You know about signals and can read what was sent from shore, so let's dispense with formality."

"Well, to be honest, Captain, I didn't manage to decipher the message."

The captain held the message before him and read.

"21.36 Fierce fighting and destruction. Tripods destroyed troops at Maybury Hill. Have halted to guard other containers that have fallen in vicinity. More armed units being deployed at Weybridge and Shepperton. Expecting new assault tomorrow."

"There's more coming in, Captain," said the signalman as a light began to flicker in pulses.

Middleton began to spell out the letters for the signalman, caught up in the excitement of the disturbing news coming from shore.

The paper was again given to the captain as he did the honours and read the message aloud.

"22.01 More tripods being assembled around Mayberry Hill and Woking. Tripods that have already engaged army are now guarding new assembly points where new containers have landed. Advance reconnaissance patrols are attacked on sight. Civilian population and Armed Forces, many killed. Exact numbers unknown. Death toll mounting. Expecting more attacks when new tripods assembled."

Commander Chudleigh looked distressed as he took a deep breath. "When do we rendezvous with *FS Courbet* and *Konig Wilhelm,* Captain?"

"0400 hours for the French, 1400 for the Germans," he replied as he looked to starboard, where lights of other vessels could be seen—all cruising parallel with *Thunder Child.* "Looks like we're acquiring company."

"I wouldn't be surprised if the entire fleet's mobilised," added Chudleigh.

"Yes French and German, too."

A sense of urgency was dawning among these men of the planet's largest Empire. Their homeland had been invaded and, with all their power and might, they were unable to stop it. The colossal navy, which had been built over centuries to defend the island, was redundant against the alien foes that fell from the oceans of space.

"Look!" Middleton pointed to the stars in dismay.

All looked up, as what looked like two shooting stars fell earthward over the dark land mass of Southern England.

"With your permission, Captain, I'll get the two sailors up on deck." Middleton felt the night was eerie now and the sea had a sinister pitch as the ironclad cut its wake through the dark mellifluous expanse—steaming into a future, black with uncertainty.

"Yes, very good, Quartermaster."

The captain turned and instructed the signalman to send a fresh message.

Indulging Mister Stanley

A bright orange sun descended westwards from the blue sky and hovered briefly above the horizon. Then gently it sank, as though relinquishing its last desperate struggle to cling to the poignant summer day. There was one last burst of splendour as the ball immersed—radiant plasma spewed into the dusk-laden sky, while seagulls cried out in their flight towards the ever-present shipping, heading eastwards.

The two signalmen of the Royal Navy stood on the lighthouse balcony, looking westwards at the spectacle and one shuddered.

"That red sky 'as never been more ominous." His Welsh accent was full of dread.

His shipmate agreed and added with his Dorset drawl, "It seems like a much fuller red—more creepy and unattractive. They call Mars the red planet and it seems we'll never look at red in the same way now."

It was at that precise moment that the principal keeper chose to step out onto the lighthouse balcony and he caught the words. Thinking the banter was meant for him to hear, he sighed and shook his head.

"Look! You lads, a joke is fine and we get the message that you don't want to let on what you're up to and all. But for God's sake, ease up with the stories now. You're flogging the blooming yarn to death."

They both looked to the principal, then to one another.

The Welsh sailor shrugged, but held his hands out in a gesture of sincerity. He raised an eyebrow then said, "With all due respect, Principal, this is not banter. You don't get much news out here on a light tower, but Britain has got something from out of space that landed in Surrey."

"He's right," added the other sailor. "It's from Mars."

"I knows what Mars is and have seen it many a time on a clear night."

"Well that's where these things are from and that man who came onto the rock with us, Mister Stanley, was nearly killed by them."

"By what?" the principal keeper cut in. He was getting rather vexed by the talk of the sailors.

"The Martians," added the Welshman. "Mister Stanley is from the War Office and his train was…"

"All right, let's not go down that path again, for God's sake. I've just about had enough of these yarns. I'll say no more, but I do understand where your Mister Stanley is coming from. So I'll keep my inquisitive mouth shut and I'll indulge him and you lads."

Before any further conversation could take place, the door opened and Salmon, flustered and excited, came out.

"There's something awful strange on land," he berated.

The others looked and frowned before walking around the balcony to the landward side. They peered through the thickening dusk towards the white chalk cliffs and could hear distant screams, as though masses of people were panicking in the gathering dimness. For several minutes they strained their ears while the dusk turned to darkness.

Suddenly, a new and unearthly noise was heard within the despairing gloom.

"Aloo, aloo." It was followed by a piercing crack that sounded like lightning—a brief glow illuminated the night sky.

"What was that?" yelled the Welsh sailor.

"It sounded like nothing earthborn to me, lad," replied the principal.

"I can hear gunfire," said Salmon. "Listen."

They all strained their ears, and leaned forward upon the balcony. The mass of distant human cries became more distinct, and there was the definite sound of sporadic gunfire.

"By God, you're right, young Salmon. What on earth is going on?" The principal peered into the thickening night and could make out a shape upon the cliff top—a distant ghostly effigy on long legs within the dusk. Just as his mind began to evaluate that, at such a distance, the mysterious thing had to be colossal, there was a blinding flash of light. A straight line of lightening shot towards them like an elongated javelin—there was a shrill screech as the bolt tore through the air. Instantly, behind them, the glass enclosure of the lighthouse erupted and glass fragments shot out in all directions. He felt the engulfing flame around him and heard the screams of his companions—one of whom he knew had been blown over the balcony as the fading scream descended down to the sea and rocks.

He was on the floor writhing, frantically trying to put out the flame and only began to calm when he heard young Salmon's voice crying out.

"Beat them out and he'll be all right."

"Use my coat!" the Welsh sailor was screaming to Salmon.

He was smothered and beaten, and the flames were suddenly gone. Then his jumbled wits began to settle as his body became alive to the cuts and burns he had sustained. There was the roar of a nearby inferno, which he knew must be the light tower. The principal turned and slowly looked up into the scorched and blooded faces of the barely recognisable Salmon and the Welsh sailor. Their matted hair was caked in congealing blood, while beyond, the red glow of fire flicked in the night sky. He was shaking with the knowledge that his person must have been as blooded and pulped as the two wretched fellows before him. How the brave men had managed to attend to his needs had been beyond him.

"Salmon. Is that you, boy?" he asked despairingly.

"Yes, Principal, and we'll need to get down and off this place. There's some machine thing on legs coming towards the light tower."

He looked out towards the coast. "God! They were telling the truth."

"Aye," said the sailor. "And the sooner we're away, the better, boyo. Come on now," he looked towards the shore anxiously. "That thing is coming over. It might fire more of the light heat and I don't rightly fancy being up here."

The principal felt helpful hands pulling him up and he cried out as embedded glass fragments moved in his ripped flesh. There were curses and hisses from Salmon and the surviving sailor, who were obviously experiencing the same discomfort. They climbed inside the lighthouse room through the wrecked framework and around the burning desolation of what had been the light tower—the heat almost forcing them back onto the balcony.

"We must get to the door, lads," barked the principal, holding up his scorched arm. The pain from the burns was almost unbearable, but the combination of fear and a will to survive drove him on. Behind him followed Salmon and the sailor, all equally in pain and driven by the same desire to live.

"Aloo, aloo." The hostile abomination was getting nearer.

All three peered back and were horrified to see a gigantic machine-creature striding across the shallow sea towards the light rock. It was like a giant daddy longlegs spider, though with three legs—its bodied trunk appeared to be off-white—almost stained. It was a fleeting glimpse that set their already strained hearts beating faster.

"Get to the stairs, for God's sake," yelled the principal.

As he reached the stairwell door, it burst open and an armed sailor came into the burning light room.

"We're coming down, lad. We've got to get off the rock now."

"How many are left, Taffy?" asked the sailor, oblivious to the principal's words.

"Only us," he answered. "Mills was blown over the balcony. You can't do anything with that." He gestured to the sailor's rifle.

"Right, get down the stairs as quick as you can," said the young able seaman to the principal and Salmon. "You go with them, Taffy."

They needed no further encouragement, though the principal and Salmon could hear the Welsh sailor pleading with his shipmate to follow. The sound of rifle fire echoing down the stairwell gave the answer of the stubborn shipmate and the rapid patter of boots following told them that the Welsh sailor had given up trying to persuade the stubborn yet brave young sailor otherwise.

A second screech ripped through the air—much louder this time—and a booming roar accompanied it, which shook the light tower to such a degree, the three fleeing men almost fell down the last part of the stairwell. They fled out the main door onto the stone steps that led down to a small rowing boat, where two more sailors were climbing into it.

All around them, cascading stone and debris was raining into the sea while each man felt compelled to look up. They gasped in horror at the sight of the wrecked and burning light tower. Then from around the tower's curve came the chilling cry that tore throughout the night, followed by the awesome sight of the gigantic tripod at terrifyingly close quarters. The hideous thing's off-white dirty trunk was much clearer and each side had green compound windows, like the eyes of a fly. None could make out whether they were artificial windows or organic orbs that protruded out of the armour casing. The flickering flames of the burning tower cast grotesque shadows upon the monstrosity as it stood before its burning devastation, like a sentinel—fresh from hell. A long arm projected from the trunk, delved into the burning light tower and rummaged within the debris as though uncannily searching for something.

There followed a petrifying human scream and, as the arm came away from the burning top the gallant sailor, who had elected to stay above and shoot at the alien, was seen frantically wriggling in a feeble and helpless effort to get free. The Martian pulled the wretched sailor across one of the green compound structures as though to stare at the contemptible little thing before it.

The machine then turned and strode back towards the shore—its gigantic legs wading through the shallow sea. It was either unaware or disinterested in the lighter crew and the remaining sailors at the bottom of the light tower.

Each survivor shuddered and lowered his head in shame at the brave sailor being carried away by the immense tripod. There was nothing anyone could do for the wretched soul. The sorrowful screams of the captured sailor gradually faded into the night, while above, the light tower roared.

"Oh my God," muttered Salmon as he nervously tried to wipe the flowing blood from his eyes. "I thought they were mucking us about when they were going on about aliens from another world."

The bloodied and burnt principal grabbed the banister rail and tried to make his way down to the boat.

"If I ever see that Mister Stanley again," he gritted his teeth as though searching for what he might say. "He was just so calm and matter-of-fact when he told us about this. I'd like to kick his bloody arse if I ever see him again."

CHAPTER 4
MORE FATIGUES

B oatswain Pickles made regular visits to the aft part of the superstructure, where Perry and Jolly were working, plaintively scraping the deck. He had shown great interest in them at Middleton's request before the man had turned in for the night. The reasons behind their circumstances were known to him and, like Middleton, he was surprised by the enormous concern the meteorite had generated. Gradually, as the night wore on, and with briefings from the captain, his intrigue had turned into stupefaction. The uncanny events were causing great concern—something that wasn't lost on Perry and Jolly because of his lack of chastisement while they were about the early morning task. They were well out of distance from hearing what the signalman was relaying to the captain and commander and, after a while, Pickles began to show less interest in them and more with the captain and his signalman. This left them free to talk, with a clear view of when he approached, plus the open sea drowned their chattering. Both accepted what was going on was of great importance—even Perry's scepticism had long been crushed. They knew they were detailed away from the rest of the crew because of what they had heard.

To the bow the day was dawning, while a vast array of battleships lay off the starboard side—some with rigging combined with steam and from many countries. Smaller vessels, mainly fishing smacks, intermingled, and the spectacle was a vast and solemn regatta, the likes of which none had ever witnessed. Everything moved eastwards, through the English Channel.

Thunder Child steamed towards the white cliffs of Dover, where the concentration of shipping was denser than anything Perry had ever imagined. He watched mystified by the unfolding events.

"Christ! I never knew there were so many ships," he muttered. "What the bloody hell is going on?"

"Bosun's on his way," hissed Jolly.

They began scraping the deck panelling a little more vigorously as Pickles ambled past the funnels, also looking out at the array of military shipping. He stopped before them.

"All right, lads." His tone was relaxed. "Captain says to have a break. You can smoke, and a steward will bring you some tea and breakfast. Seems on this occasion, little guttersnipes like you have to be waited on. Can't have you in the mess rumour-mongering now, can we?"

"No, Bosun," they replied.

He was about to continue, when Perry's open-mouthed look of surprise caused him to turn and look back past the bridge and beyond the bow, where a French battleship was falling way along the starboard bow.

"What the blazes…?" Pickles couldn't contain his surprise.

"It's a Froggie," added Jolly, equally bemused as he watched. The vessel's tricolour of blue, white and red fluttered vigorously in the sea breeze.

"*FS Courbet*! The biggest central battery ship afloat, my boys," Pickles remarked with a touch of veneration.

Perry and Jolly were in awe as the French ship fell abeam, noting her top main deck was as high as *Thunder Child*'s superstructure. She retained something of the majesty of the old sailing ships, looking colossal next to their little ironclad.

Thunder Child's bow and stern were only about eight, maybe nine, feet above sea level. However, standing on the superstructure, Perry, Jolly and the boatswain were offered an almost level view. They watched as the French crewmen moved swiftly about their duties while both vessels slowly moved together, like a couple of courting sea monsters in slow mating ritual.

"She's a strange looking thing," said Perry, noticing the prominent ram bows, which made the beam about her waterline come out to cover a wider area than her open deck.

"I reckon she capsized when they were building her," joked Jolly. "Then, on account of being French and artistic, the designers decided to put the funnels, masts and everything else that normally goes on deck, upon the hull."

"She's only got one funnel," stated Perry.

"Keep your eyes peeled, guttersnipe. You'll be no good on watch," scolded Pickles. "*FS Courbet* has two funnels standing side-by-side."

As Perry scrutinised more closely, he realised the boatswain was correct. She was an impressive but extraordinary-looking vessel that couldn't fail to turn heads. Amidships, an armoured redoubt protruded from the deck, coming out to the swollen beam's water line width, like an old castle tower. Forward and aft of the redoubt, big gun barrels extended menacingly, enabling the ship to fire directly in both directions.

"Look at her guns," said Perry.

"I'd still put money on our revolving turrets any day," answered Jolly.

"Good lad," Pickles was pleased. "They're more of a land-loving race nowadays and I don't like their ships. Don't think they'd be any good in a fight."

Perry was certain he wouldn't like to come up against the formidable vessel in battle, and was glad they were all on the same side, though he thought it prudent not to mention this before the extremely patriotic Boatswain Pickles.

Sailors of both ships ran about at the double in preparation, while the ironclads drew ever closer, but slowly—very cautiously.

The captain came out of the bridge with Commander Chudleigh and called to Pickles. "Have your two men stay there, Bosun."

"Yes, Captain."

McIntosh and his number one walked to the conning tower and descended a ladder way into the steering position, coming out by the starboard bulwark amidships. They watched as the two vessels slowly drew closer, beam to beam and then made their way to the forward turret. Here they stopped before the ladders that led down to the bow, where sailors watched over the halyard as it ran from the capstan, allowing four anchors to plunge into the sea with a resounding splash. The running chain

clanked protesting as it ran through the holds of
the bow out and around, through the hawse pipe
and following the anchors into the Channel's murky
depths.

"So this is the first rendezvous, Captain," said
Chudleigh. He surveyed the other ships in the
Channel, but couldn't recognise the German vessel
Konig Wilhelm.

"Looking for the German vessel, Number One?"

"Yes, I know the rendezvous isn't yet, but I
thought she might be around."

"No, we're to meet them off Sheerness at the
appointed time," replied McIntosh.

"Turfrey is on his way, Captain."

He looked aft and saw the lieutenant coming
along the guardrail from the roundhouse, where
the officers' quarters were. The young officer's uniform was in pristine condition, and McIntosh surmised the stewards would have been taking special
care that Turfrey went over to the French ship looking as smart as possible.

"Good morning, Turfrey," said the captain. He
had never met the man, apart from seeing him in
the waiting room yesterday afternoon when they
had disembarked. The War Office had given orders
to McIntosh only a few hours before boarding the
vessel, choosing the young officer as a liaison to the
French.

"Morning, sir," replied Turfrey.

"We're making an exchange with the French, as you know. For your services, the *FS Courbet* is sending us a Lieutenant Devour. I hope you'll do us credit, Turfrey."

"I'll do my absolute best, sir."

McIntosh smiled, then replied. "I'm sure you will. Well, you'll be going over to the *Courbet* in a moment."

The three officers watched as the French vessel's port neared their starboard bulwarks.

"She's an impressive old bird, Captain." Chudleigh liked the powerful looking ram bow. It reminded him of pictures he had seen of Greek and Roman galleys when they had docked in Italy.

Suddenly from above, there came a mild commotion and all looked up towards the open part of the bridge where Boatswain Pickles was poised on one of the ladder ways that led down onto the top of the fore gun's turret. He was presumably conversing with Lieutenant Faulbs, who was inside the bridge house.

"Will do right away, sir," they heard him call. He looked down to the captain and descended the ladder, passing from view as he went to another ladder at the back of the turret. He appeared from behind holding a note to the captain.

"New signals from the shore station, sir."

McIntosh took the note and frowned. "Is this all there was, Bosun?"

"Afraid so, sir. We did ask and so did the other vessels all about, but it seems communications to Dover are cut. They just keep saying the same thing, sir."

"This is getting worse by the minute," muttered McIntosh.

"What's happened now, sir?" Chudleigh looked to Pickles as the captain answered.

"Weybridge and Shepperton have been destroyed with enormous loss of life. There appears to be total panic, and refugees are converging on London and making for the coastline in droves." He handed the note to Chudleigh. "Sooner or later, I'm going to have to let the crew know what's going on. The men must realise something is up by all this." McIntosh nodded his head to the *FS Courbet*, the ships and boats beyond that littered the Channel.

Chudleigh nodded. "I think it might be a good idea, sir." He looked down onto the bow section, where sailors were working by the halyard. The men were uneasy. It was noticeable at a glance.

"We'll sort this out and then I'll assemble the crew to debrief them," said the captain, finally committed. "When I've done that, you can relieve the two men in your charge, Bosun. They've been up all night. It won't do any harm to let them sleep."

"Yes, sir. If I may, I'd like to go back aloft and stand with them until they're dismissed."

"Very good, Bosun, see to it."

A Visit from Mister Stanley

Mrs Wade jolted as she looked out her front room window. Flustered, the house-proud widow pushed back her auburn hair and brushed down her apron. It was most unusual to get visitors—especially male ones. Suddenly, she had three! A middle-aged, balding man in spectacles, accompanied by two armed sailors were walking up her garden path towards the house. She'd been watching the shipping from the front window when, to her surprise, the visitors had appeared at her front gate.

"Oh my word. What will the neighbours think?" she muttered. "How strange." It had been the most peculiar of mornings with hordes of people coming along from the western approach into Herne Bay. In fact, she had never seen so many in all her life and, at first, thought the town might have been holding a summer fair she hadn't heard about. However, in each passing face she noticed anxiety, and realised that something dreadful must have happened and that every one of them was just passing through. She desired to know, but didn't dare venture out because some of the travellers looked desperate to degrees she considered extreme.

She left the window and went to the front door just as the loud knock came. She opened it to see the very pleasant little bald-headed man smiling at her. His general demeanour was that of a man who was usually smart, but for some reason, was now dishevelled.

"Good day, madam, I'm so sorry to trouble you. My name is Albert Stanley and I am from the War Office."

"Oh, indeed," she replied, regarding the two armed sailors suspiciously. "What can I do for you, Mister Stanley?"

"We need to go up into your loft, madam, and gain access to the roof. We want to set up a semaphore and your house has a clear view of the sea, plus the old ruined abbey at Reculver."

He pointed east to the far off jutting, white chalk cliff, upon which stood the distant ruins. "We need to signal to vessels at sea and liaise with the Reculver semaphore along the coast."

"Can't you do that at the top of the cliff road?" she asked nervously. "It's higher and you can still…"

"There are too many refugees along the cliff road, madam. It will hamper us. They're trying to get to Margate, Ramsgate and Broadstairs."

"Why? What's wrong?"

"You haven't been in touch with affairs of late, madam?"

"No, I don't go out much and I don't read the papers."

"Please, madam, may we enter? It is of the utmost importance and I'll enlighten you as to what is happening." He gave her a gentle smile, which she found settling.

Mrs Wade opened the door and allowed the unexpected visitors in. Another smile settled upon his face, which exuded charm while observing the simple yet neat way the cottage was kept. She found Mister Stanley's silent endorsement very welcoming and knew there was something about the man she could warm to.

"Is your husband at work?"

"I'm a widow, Mister Stanley," she replied.

"Oh, I'm so sorry…"

"Mrs Wade," she added.

"I'm very sorry, Mrs Wade."

She sighed. "It's been seven years now, Mister Stanley." She looked at the two navy men and decided there was nothing ill with the visitors. "You can go upstairs to the loft. You'll find stepladders in the wall closet beneath the hatch."

They smiled their appreciation and left her with Mister Stanley. She felt suddenly shy in front of the important-looking man.

"So you don't know what is going on then, Mrs Wade?" he asked.

"Well, all the people look as though they're fleeing and I felt awkward going out among them to ask. Has there been a fire or something? It can't be Whitstable. We would have seen the smoke."

"No, Mrs Wade, I'm afraid to say it's far more serious than that. Far more serious, indeed." He looked around the place again and enjoyed the charming neatness. The place and the lady had a welcoming attraction, which, for once in his life, he wasn't afraid of. "Have you lived here all your life, Mrs Wade?"

"Yes," she replied and went into the kitchen, motioning him to follow. "I suppose you could say I've lived a fairly sheltered life, even more so with the passing of my husband."

She filled the kettle with water and took it to the stove, then got out the teapot and tipped the old leaves down the sink.

"So you're not even aware of anything falling from the sky in Surrey?" he asked as she pottered about making tea.

"Oh, I did hear about that. I clean a pub during closing hours. Brings that little extra against my widow's pension. Well, the landlady said that something had fallen on a common near Woking. What on earth she meant, I don't know."

"That is the root cause of this trouble, Mrs Wade."

She listened as Mister Stanley told her of what had happened, and appeared concerned while pouring out the tea, but she still couldn't quite take on the enormity of the situation. Martian tripods sounded very impressive, but they were a long way away and she couldn't quite picture what the colossal outer-world creatures looked like. Mister Stanley soon realised she had no concept of the fact that she lived on a round world and that space had other round worlds with creatures living upon them. Poor Mrs Wade had never needed to know, for her world was her little cottage and beyond was Herne Bay. She'd ventured the few miles to Margate on occasions during her travelling days, but beyond that, nothing.

"Were you born here, Mrs Wade?" he asked politely as she put the cup of tea in front of him.

"Yes," she smiled. "The place was my mother and father's. When they passed on, I took the rent over. Well, my late husband and me, that is." She put two cups on a tray with a sugar bowl and a plate of biscuits, then took them up to the sailors, who were busy setting up the semaphore.

Albert Stanley watched as she left the kitchen. He smiled to himself and shook his head. "Dear Mrs Wade. Your poor little world is about to be turned upside down." How would she cope? Who would look out for her? She was such a wonderful lady of simple pleasures, and his heart began to flutter because soon the fighting machines would come and beautiful Herne Bay would be rubble and fire and the pretty seaside town would become a twisted and defiled landscape.

"Oh dear," he whispered to himself. "Poor Mrs Wade."

CHAPTER 5

THE SECRET OF THUNDER CHILD

Perry sighed as he was about to climb into his hammock.

"I don't care what blooming things are meant to be rampaging around the countryside. Martians or no Martians, I'm for some shuteye. I feel whacked and it's all down to your blooming laughing gear flexing muscles, when it should've been shut."

Jolly frowned. "Do you mean because I shot me mouth off you're whacked? Or the Martians are here to shut me up personally?"

"What the blooming heck are you on about now?"

"It's the way you put things, Perry. You can be unwittingly entertaining at times."

Perry grinned forcefully, trying to hide his agitation. Jolly could be infuriating, but the man often made jokes that went over his head. His response was often to remain silent and ride much of the banter directed at him.

"When it comes to wit, you're not exactly the sharpest knife in the drawer, are you, me old fruit?" Jolly had seen through him long ago and was now exercising his cruel streak. After all, Perry was a fresh young boy seaman, wet behind the ears and ripe for a little leg pulling.

"You're really asking for it." Perry's face became serious and he walked towards Jolly menacingly. "Now I'm telling you—knock it off. I've had enough since leaving port to last me a lifetime."

"Oh my word! What's the likes of you going to do about it then?" Jolly grinned irritatingly. "God, you are taking liberties. Fancy trying to sling your weight about with me. You! A fresh-faced seventeen-year old." Maybe he should have a little fun with the youngster, put him in his place. "I'm hardening you, boy. You'll be able to ride this sort of thing from others by the time I'm finished with you, so I think you should be thanking me for the ridicule I'm taking time to visit upon you. It's making you tougher and stronger of character."

Perry looked aghast and began to chomp at the bit, much to his antagonist's amusement. "You can't be serious! You bloody..." He stopped as Jolly's ugly sneer fell over his guileless response, washing away the futile words that would have followed.

Chuckling away, Jolly went on. "I likes you, Perry, and I'm being a friend. I'm strengthening your character."

"You must be a good friend indeed for doing something like that, Jolly. A real mate." He was no longer irate. A calm had swept over him. "So I'm going to do something for you to improve your integrity."

"What, a young recruit like you? Come on, Perry, me boy—what could you possibly teach me?"

Jolly found out instantly as the youngster's fist caught him smartly in the mouth. The impact produced an explosion in his eardrums, causing a momentary blackness as he was sent spinning onto the ladder and banging his forehead. A second punch caught him in the left kidney while he was still searching for his incoherent wits. It served to bring him from his concussion, where he would have been happy to remain, for he awoke into a world of pain. Nauseating affliction in the small of his back, a top lip that had his incisors buried into it and a headache from the metal ladder he had smashed into. Before he could make any remonstrations of peace, he was pulled away from the ladder to face his young opponent.

Perry was not the soft touch he had taken him for and now the youngster was displaying a quality he had dreadfully underestimated. Jolly was useless and unable to offer any reasonable resistance, except a feeble attempt to strike back. The blow was easily parried, then Perry struck again, catching him squarely on the nose. A creek burst within his head as though the noise was smashing its way out of his ears. He reeled back, vaguely accepting his nose was broken before stumbling over a table.

Other seamen came quickly to stop the fight and Jolly felt helping hands pull him to his feet.

"All right, mate, I think you've taught him a lesson," said one of the older sailors—a brusque looking man in his late thirties, though once he spoke, he came across as very amiable.

"If he thinks he's ready to lay off, then that's fine by me," replied Perry. "But let's hear from the man himself. I've been on fatigues all night on account of that bastard and he don't know when to keep his big mouth shut."

Jolly stood, blood oozing from his mouth and broken nose, clearly shaken by his ordeal, accepting that the seventeen-year-old boy seaman was anything but ordinary. He pulled his arm away from the sailor who had helped him up and walked off sulking.

"He's off to the washroom to clean himself up. Then he can go to sick bay to get dressings from his accidental nasty fall."

Perry was reassured by the old sailor's words. He looked like a person who knew the ropes and it was comforting to be in such company.

"Thanks, mate," said Perry, full of gratitude. A friend was what he really needed now and the old hand had the makings of a decent person.

"No problem. New, ain't you?"

"Yeah. Does it show that much?"

"Course it does, but you can't let that bother you. We're all new at one time or another."

"I arrived four days ago and this is my first voyage."

The old sailor smiled. "I've seen you about. You were in the tavern on Thursday night when the salesman was talking about meteorites and how they land all the time."

"He certainly got it all wrong," laughed Perry nervously. He climbed into his hammock. "What do you think of all this?"

The old hand snorted as though he didn't know whether to be confused or amused. "Beats me. I've never heard anything so bloody ludicrous in my life." He was about to leave Perry to get some sleep, but was stopped as he turned.

"What's your name, mate?"

"Fancourt. Harry Fancourt."

"I'm Albert Perry."

"Pleased to meet you, Albert," grinned Fancourt, holding out a hand.

"Likewise, Harry. What do you do?"

He pointed to the badge on his arm. "One of the gun crew."

"Ever fired in anger?"

"A few times, but not on *Thunder Child.*"

"When?"

"East Africa. Dhows—Arab slave ships. Not much opposition from them. Quick shot across the bow and they're usually stopped. Sometimes, we would put a shell into one if they didn't heed the first shot."

"Nothing beyond that?" Perry seemed disappointed.

"The Royal Navy hasn't been challenged for some time now. Most of the Empire's confrontations come from land-based enemies."

"Maybe we'll come up against these Martian things."

"Not in this old tub. She's a bit past it," laughed Fancourt. "I reckon the bigger ships are going to be doing most of the heavy work. We're nothing more than observation. *Thunder Child*'s far too outdated for this sort of thing. She was on her way to the knacker's yard when this emergency happened. The most powerful navy in the world is hardly likely to sling an antiquated ship with muzzle-loading guns at any enemy."

"If we're so old and past it, why did they bother keeping her for so long, and what use would she be now?" Perry was puzzled.

"She's nothing more than a coastal defence vessel. Even if she's a bit big for such. I reckon they should have refitted her years ago, but for some reason, poor old *Thunder Child* has had no attention at all. She spends her time lurking in harbours and sailing around the coastline. Done so for years now. This appointing of the new captain is probably one of the most unusual events to happen in her history."

"Well I think she's a ship that carries something special," said Perry. He liked the ironclad with its main deck and superstructure that extended to the sides, supporting the base of the turrets before the recessed forward and aft decks.

"Oh she's a good old bird," agreed Fancourt. "Her freeboard sits a bit low for my liking, but I agree, she has an aura about her. At the bow below the sea level, she's got a wicked little ram that can pack quite a punch, I would reckon. Boy, I'd dearly love to see her use that ram one day. Would be a sight to behold indeed."

"Why is it that *Thunder Child* is so obscure and unnoticed by the Admiralty then? There must be a reason."

"Well," began Fancourt, looking down at the floor. "She was built at a time when there was unrest in the corridors of power. Ironclads were in their infancy and many retained sail, as well as their boilers. There were arguments about turret ships and central batteries. All sorts of architects put forward designs for better vessels and one such person was a Captain Cowper Phipps Coles, who designed and built a turret ship called *HMS Captain*. Her freeboard was only eight and a half feet above sea level with these turret bases resting on them. She also had sails to take her out into the high seas. It was argued that she was top heavy and unstable by the Admiralty's Chief Constructor, a man called Reed. This argument became quite heated and it's well known that the two men took their disagreement to the top. Anyway, Coles got his way and the ship was launched, even with a freeboard lower than the original eight and a half feet. At first, she seemed alright, passing various tests for seaworthiness and then one day in the Bay of Biscay, she sank during windy weather, taking most of the crew, including Coles."

"God, that's a dreadful story. When did this happen?" Perry was engrossed by the old seaman's tale.

"1871, barely a year before Reed's *HMS Devastation* was launched. She was the first ship to do away with sail and rigging, but her turrets were that of Coles' design, even though the court-martial concluded the demise of *HMS Captain* was due to the private design having many faults. One of them was rumoured to be the weight of the gun turrets, though it's only gossip, you understand. Other things were mentioned, like the masts being too boisterous. Top heavy things, you see, which all added to her instability."

"Well it's all very interesting, but where does *Thunder Child* fit into this tale of intrigue?" Perry was becoming impatient.

"I'm just coming to that. Well, it's like this, you see. This *HMS Devastation* did have Coles' turret design and because of it, his widow was paid royalties. This ship come about a few years later because someone in the Admiralty had the design and go ahead ready and it had some of Cole's other designs added after his death, much to the anger of others in the construction department, including Reed, who had moved on.

"One of the men who forwarded the plan was said to have been present at the court of inquiry and was rather scathing about private designers challenging the navy's projects. However, he allowed this ship to be built, contrary to what he said and when it was found out in the corridors of power, it was swept under the carpet and *Thunder Child* was confined to low-key duties and kept out of harm's way. They tried to sell her, but were stopped."

"How do you know things like this?" Perry was only a boy seaman, but he knew a gunner shouldn't be privy to such information.

"Like you and Jolly, I have overheard officers talking about her."

"So *Thunder Child* is a neglected ship then."

"She is at that, me lad. Look at her. A fine ship she is, but still with muzzle-loading guns. *Devastation* had a sister ship launched a few years later and when she had an accident with her muzzle-loading guns the navy did away with them and renovated ships with breech loaders. Not *Thunder Child* though! She was left. I'm honestly surprised she hasn't been scrapped before now, and when she finally was supposed to be, she wins a reprieve. Maybe fate has ordained that she be earmarked for something special, aye, lad."

"You make it seem as though she's an embarrassment, some sort of skeleton in the cupboard."

"She is lad, to those in office in London. Men who never come to see her."

"Bet she's still got some clout," laughed Perry.

Fancourt chuckled too. "A-ho you can be sure, lad. I bet she could give a likely account of herself, all right. Even with her muzzle-loaded guns in this advanced day and age, she can pack a punch and if anyone stops one of her shells—they're not going to feel lucky because it wasn't fired from a breech-loaded gun, now are they?"

"No, I don't think they'd feel lucky at all," agreed Perry laughing.

"Get some shut eye, boy. I'll have a word with Quartermaster Middleton, if you like. Get his consent to take you around the ship properly and see if you can have a look at the guns."

"That would be great," said Perry. "Thanks, Harry." He watched as the gunnery man walked off. Secretly, he felt pleased with himself—his blood was still rushing from the confrontation with Jolly, but he had come out squarely on top of matters.

The Wisdom of Mister Stanley

"They're coming, Mister Stanley," yelled the young sailor, who came crashing down the stairs as if all hell's minions were hot on his tail.

"Good Lord!" replied Mister Stanley softly, which brought about a calming air. The effect on the young sailor was immediate. "Wait here with Mrs Wade." He looked to her and gently smiled. "I'll be but a moment."

Though initially shaken by the excitable sailor, she had become composed at Mister Stanley's manner. "Could I come, too? If I am to see what these things look like, it might as well be now."

Outside, the buzz of alarm could be heard by the fleeing refugees—their excitable pitch electrified the atmosphere to such a degree, all in Mrs Wade's cottage felt the ripples of despair.

Mister Stanley smiled and, not wanting to offend the woman, he nodded his head, while inside his mother's voice was scolding him.

"What on Earth are you thinking, Albert? She's a gentlewoman."

He shut the vision from his mind with a parting thought. *Not now, Mother.*

All three trudged up the stairs and then climbed the ladder into the loft. Once through the roof's skylight, the noise of the fleeing masses was deafening. To the rear of the terraced cottage, beyond the small yards, rose a grassy slope, atop of which was a road packed with people all hurrying to be out of Herne Bay.

"Look!" cried out the other signalman who had remained. He pointed west over the seaside town's rooftops, then turned east to the ruined abbey at Reculver, and began sending flag signals.

They watched in complete horror, as beyond the town's rooftops, a titanic, vile deformity approached the eastern fringes of Herne Bay. Its metallic legs glittered in the afternoon sun as it moved forward forebodingly with intrepidly wicked grace. It was an evil, yet sublime, vision of power, which infringed and blighted the resplendent beauty of the typically English summer meadows and seaside town of Herne

Bay—awesome, magnificent and detestable. The white armoured body trunk above the long, jointed legs turned lazily from right to left as its compound orbs scanned the surrounding approaches. There appeared to be a meshed exterior vein-like structure around the machine's leg joints. These were transparent and had a plasma-like liquid flowing through them. They fed into one thicker vein that ran up and down each leg's length and it was difficult to fathom whether this was lubricant or organic plasma.

"Aloo!"

The high-pitched scream emitted from the fighting machine as a long, artificial tentacle emerged from the trunk, at the end of which was a cylinder. A ripping crack like that of lightning spanned out like a menacing ripple as a flash of light shot out, rupturing a rooftop within the town's centre. Slate and brick were cast in all directions, coupled with the roar of falling debris. Screams of panic emerged from the distant street and the sound of neighing horses mingled within the terrified despair.

"Oh my God," muttered Mrs Wade as she put her hands to her mouth.

"All off the roof now," ordered Mister Stanley as he took Mrs Wade by the hand.

"I need to stay and keep contact with Reculver," said one of the sailors. He looked to the younger seaman, who was clearly terrified. "You stay with Mister Stanley, do you understand?"

The younger sailor needed no second bidding and he was hot upon the heels of Mister Stanley and Mrs Wade. In the background, there were the further sounds of the light ray ripping through the air and the roar of exploding buildings amid the cries of human pandemonium. They had been on the roof for about thirty seconds and had seen enough of the terrifying Martians to last a lifetime.

"What are we going to do, Mister Stanley?" stuttered Mrs Wade, clearly frightened.

"Is the coal bunker in the yard?"

"Yes."

"Is it empty?"

"Almost. There's not much call for it in summer."

"That's good, Mrs Wade." He turned to the sailor, who was descending the loft ladder. "You and Mrs Wade hide in the coal bunker, but first you must do exactly as I say. Get wet rags, anything will do. Dampen them and wrap coal in them, then hold them to your mouth. The black smoke might not penetrate the bunker, but if it does, you might be alright breathing through damp coal."

"Aren't we running with the rest?" the young sailor was concerned.

"No! That thing will follow the masses and blanket the poor souls with black gas. It is toxic and kills in massive numbers. There is nothing that can be done for them and I won't be heard above the panic. Stay and hide until it passes. Do you understand?"

"Yes, sir," he replied.

"Take Mrs Wade now."

"What will you do, Mister Stanley?" asked Mrs Wade passively.

"I need to be with the signalman. I want to make sure he comes down as soon as he can. Then we will come to the bunker, too. If we don't make it, you must not open the doors for a long time—do you understand? It is vital that you comply with what I am saying."

"Please be careful," she called as the young sailor took her gently by the arm and led her downstairs. She began to cry, while outside, the forsaken masses screamed in panic and tried to run.

Mister Stanley got to the roof as more explosions went off in the town centre. The Martian machine-creature was wading amid the rooftops, firing at random and laying a blanket of thick, black smoke. People could be seen coming out of streets and pelting towards the beach, screaming in panic. Men, women and children, even dogs and horses. It was terrifying and Mister Stanley hung his head in shame because there was nothing he could do.

"Oh my God," he muttered.

The signalman knelt beside him and looked in dismay as the masses swarmed into the sea. A black cloud that drifted over their line of vision obscured the wretched people.

Suddenly, the sailor gripped Mister Stanley's arm. "The black smoke is coming this way. It's killing people." He could see some of the town's folk falling in agonised panic, clutching their throats before the black smog obscured their withering forms.

"Quick, lad, follow me now." Mister Stanley had become calm and authoritative again. He led the way back down into the attic and then the hallway.

"What are we going to do?" asked the sailor, clearly petrified.

Mister Stanley grabbed two armchair coverings from the lounge, then ran into the kitchen and plunged them into the dirty dishwater Mrs Wade hadn't had time to empty.

"Into the yard, quickly."

They fled out back and ran to the coal bunker, while beyond the yard fence the tumult of fleeing people became even more high-pitched. In the distance, the machine-creature cried out and the air splitting screech of the heat-ray could be heard, combined with another explosion. As they opened the lid of the bunker to see the pitiable forms of Mrs Wade and the younger sailor cuddling in fear, the first signs of black toxic mist drifted over the yard shed, to the side of which was a small rowing boat.

"Put the coal to your mouths and breathe through it," yelled Mister Stanley as he and the older sailor got in and slammed the lid firmly shut. His mind was racing ahead of things that were happening and he was thinking of the aftermath, when all the abominations had rolled over and all had to move on.

The boat! He remembered the boat as they trembled in their claustrophobic, dank domain, knowing that outside, the toxic gas lingered.

CHAPTER 6
THROUGH THE STRAIGHTS OF DOVER

Captain McIntosh had debriefed Lieutenant Devour about events on shore and the French liaison officer was clearly astonished by the facts. He knew the meteorites were causing panic in Britain, but didn't appreciate the true significance of what had actually been happening. His own captain was equally bewildered upon hearing the British reports, and he surmised the British liaison officer, now departed to his ship, was debriefing the other officers of *FS Courbet* in their waiting room. These officers, no doubt, would be wearing those same dismayed looks.

"Hard to take in, isn't it, Lieutenant Devour?" said Commander Chudleigh.

"It is very difficult to grasp, sir. Very difficult indeed." His English was almost perfect, with just the slightest hint of an accent.

"It becomes more bloody bizarre with every signal we receive from the shoreline communications," added the captain as he turned from the signalman standing by the semaphore. He looked out at the array of shipping that swarmed in the Channel—vessels of every shape and size clogging the sea-lanes.

"I keep expecting to wake up out of a weird dream," agreed the Frenchman. "And can only wonder what these things look like."

The signalman called.

"Another message, sir."

He was standing on a small platform that went out from the superstructure to hang out above the freeboard, almost into the open sea. Bulwark safety rails surrounded him and he called back as he began to read the message.

The three officers moved to the bulwarks, where the suspended lifeboat hung outboard from gantries. They peered at the coastline as flag signals were hoisted high above the passing white cliff tops.

"Martians are consolidating and attending new cylinders that have fallen from space," began the signalman. "More tripods are expected to be constructed. Any attempts of surveillance are dealt with swiftly by heat-ray or toxic gas. Artillery units deployed on the outskirts of London. Population getting restless and some heading for the eastern coastal towns. Suggest that men aboard ships take damp cloth or handkerchief with lump of coal from stokeholds. Wrap inside and use as a crude gasmask. Gunners of an artillery unit survived a tripod gas attack by inhaling through such devices."

Commander Chudleigh looked to starboard, where other battleships took aboard the same information. "Well that's something I suppose, but it won't stop heat-rays."

"Blast," commented Captain McIntosh. "We can no longer send our own messages now with so many other ships of the fleet here. Only *HMS Caesar* can send in."

"We'll have to hope she asks questions we would like, worst luck." Chudleigh spoke like a schoolboy, who has been denied a second helping of pudding.

"Can you not relay through *Caesar*?" asked Lieutenant Devour.

Chudleigh looked at him. "Oh we can, old chap, but then so does every other ship in the fleet. *Caesar* will only select ones she likes after her own questions are answered."

"Let's leave the big boys to play, shall we?" The captain walked off, leaving Chudleigh and Devour with the signalman. He ducked beneath the stress wires connected to the fore funnel and went into the hatch that entered the rear of the bridge. He had seen and heard enough from the offshore communications and it was clear he should proceed with the next part of his schedule. He called out new navigation settings and an increase in speed to Faulbs, who in return relayed the orders through the voice pipe to the wheelhouse and the engine room.

Looking out the observation window on the open bridge balcony, the captain felt a sense of contentment as the bow sliced through the surf, passed the Straights of Dover and went into the North Sea. Even in the moderate conditions, the waves smashed over the forecastle as the sturdy ironclad's engines propelled her onwards.

Chudleigh opened the door and allowed Devour to enter the bridge, while he remained by the hatchway. "Captain, should I act on the advice of the wet cloth and coal?"

"Yes, Number One. See to it, would you?"

"Very good, sir." He left to attend to the matter.

Lieutenant Devour stood beside him and watched the vessel smash into the waves—sending its spray all over the forecastle. The bow of the British ship was much lower than the *FS Courbet's*, which seemed much less sturdy to him, but then again, there was something about the little coastal defence ironclad that he liked. What, he couldn't say, but there was a sleekness as the vessel sliced into the green glut, shattering it into a white bilge that was thrown in all directions. Much of it washed across the bow around the capstan and chains, then spilled off the sides and through the hawse pipes.

"Where are we to go now, Captain?" he asked.

"We're to continue to a location where the German vessel *Konig Wilhelm* will meet us, and then we will take aboard one of their liaison officers. It's developing into quite an outing, wouldn't you agree, Lieutenant?"

"I would indeed, Captain."

"Ever seen the *Konig Wilhelm*?"

"No, sir, but I hear she's a fine ship."

"Oh she is, a very splendid ship indeed. Had an unfortunate accident a few years back in these very waters when she accidentally rammed another of her vessels, *Grosser Kurfurst*. Sunk her with the loss of around five hundred lives."

"Yes, I heard the story. It happened twenty years ago."

They both fell silent, realising their idle chit-chat wasn't lifting the mood, which was falling over the bridge like a dark shadow.

The captain was lost in a trance, wondering about the Martian tripods. He was certain he would see one in time and then the reality hiding behind a cloud of suggestion would, perhaps, become plain.

Sometimes, he imagined it might be an elaborate exercise—a fantastic training schedule that had been kept top secret, but deep down, he knew all that was happening was real. He felt the ship was doomed, cruising towards an ominous inevitability as the bow sank and lifted, cutting its way towards the dark horizon. Beyond, destiny waited, enticing like an alluring lady of ill repute and *Thunder Child*, like a wonderfully shallow man, followed anyway.

"Do you think we will see these tripods, Captain?" Devour could almost have been reading his thoughts.

"I have the firm belief we will, Lieutenant. I want to fire *Thunder Child*'s guns at one, and I have the strangest of premonitions that we will."

"Pardon me for saying, Captain, but I couldn't help noticing the short barrels that protrude from *Thunder Child*'s turrets. They're old muzzle-loaders, which I was led to believe were obsolete in the Royal Navy of today."

"You're right, Lieutenant, and it must be obvious to you that this is an antiquated coastal defence ship. Expendable, but still able to deliver a punch if required."

Devour never pursued his questions. It would have been too impolite and obvious—*Thunder Child* was ready for the scrap heap and money wasted on breech-loading guns would be better spent elsewhere. She must have won some sort of respite due to the emergency that had occurred. He was slightly uneasy at the captain's use of the word 'expendable', however. What did he know and why was he so sure they would face the alien tripods?

Outside, other battleships of Britain, France and Germany cruised amid the flotilla of yachts and steamers. Every vessel headed along the Kent coast northward towards the mouth of the Thames estuary. Never in the world's history had there ever been such a clamour of ships, and amid them all, he sensed the mighty little ironclad *Thunder Child* was marked for a purpose. An aspiration that made all the huge monsters of floating iron with their big breech-loading guns nothing to what the plucky ship would be.

"Do you believe in fate, Captain?" asked Devour.

"Usually, I'm the cynical Scot, as my fellow Britons might say, but today! Right now, I do."

"Do the English believe their fellow Britons so?" Devour smiled, he hadn't realised that Captain McIntosh was Scottish. He looked at Faulbs, who wore an amused smile.

The captain looked too, and smiled. "Perhaps you could answer that for Lieutenant Devour," he smirked.

"Not at all," laughed Faulbs. "We have the utmost respect."

The bridge's atmosphere became a little more light-hearted and the captain left them in jovial spirits, going out the back hatchway, passing the fore funnel and down the ladder in the conning tower to the wheelhouse. He asked the steersman if all was well.

"All's well, Captain."

He went out onto the starboard side of the main deck and along the bulwark to the fore turret, where Gunner Fancourt was standing with young Seaman Perry, one of the men who had overheard him talking to Chudleigh about the crisis.

They both stood to attention as he approached and the captain stopped, interested in what was going on.

"Name," he ordered.

"Gunner Fancourt, Captain."

McIntosh looked to Perry with a stern eye.

"Boy Seaman Perry, Captain," said Perry.

"As you were." He replied knowing the sailors were hard pushed to stand to attention on the rolling freeboard. They thankfully grabbed the guardrail.

"So what's all this then, Gunner Fancourt?" The captain's manner was pleasant and inquisitive.

"Just showing the lad around the guns, sir. The quartermaster thinks a small induction would be useful to the lad, sir."

"Indeed it would, Gunner Fancourt. Have you ever fired these type of guns?"

"I have, sir."

"Recently, I mean."

"I have fired these very guns during a training session about three weeks ago, sir," replied Fancourt. "But I've also fired them on other occasions, sir."

McIntosh was interested. "So a few men, including yourself, have had a little experience with old muzzle-loaders."

"We have, sir."

"And all these men are still aboard?"

"Yes, sir."

"Who took you for this training session?"

"Commander Scott, sir."

"Commander Percy Scott," thought McIntosh as things began to make sense and the mist began to clear. More and more, he was convinced the ship had a purpose—things began to grow alarmingly disturbing. He frowned, deep in thought for a few moments, before looking back at Fancourt.

"Carry on, Gunner Fancourt," he smiled and went back along the freeboard, passed the rear turret and descended the central ladder way onto the quarterdeck and then into the hatchway beneath the stairs. He saw Chief Steward Doherty and asked for Chudleigh to be sent to his cabin as soon as possible.

As he entered his quarters, the armchair in front of his desk looked very inviting and more comfortable than his writing chair. He went to the drinks cabinet and poured himself a whisky, leaving an empty glass ready for when Chudleigh arrived, then he sank into the armchair. There were other seats about the room and the commander would have to content himself with one of those. He was taking the comfy armchair, no matter what. He took a generous sip of whisky and reclined his head as the liquid warmed his throat, then sighed satisfactorily as his mind reclined into thinking on the issue of gunnery and what Fancourt had just told him about the gun training. He would have dearly liked to question the gunner further, but then it would be sound to think Chudleigh was aboard during the training exercise.

Commander Percy Scott was a name known to him, and the fact he had been training the gunners aboard *Thunder Child* intrigued him somewhat. *Why train the crew of an old ship with obsolete muzzle-loading guns?* He took another sip of whisky and listened to the propellers gyrating just below the floor, where the keel's curve accommodated them.

"It doesn't make sense, damn it," he cursed.

There came a knock.

"Come in," he called as the door swung open to reveal Chudleigh.

"Told you wanted to see me, Captain."

"Yes, come in, Number One. Help yourself to a drink."

"Thank you, sir." He needed no second invitation and poured himself a generous measure of whisky.

"Take a seat," said McIntosh, and Chudleigh quickly complied, thanking him as he did.

"I've got a few questions simmering in my mind," he continued.

"Oh." Chudleigh was a little concerned as he took a sip of his drink. When a captain was worried and called him aside to ask questions, one never knew where it might lead.

"This ship was taken on a gunnery exercise three weeks ago, is that correct?"

"Yes, sir, it was with Commander Scott. Why do you ask? Is it important?"

"Do you know the results of the test that were conducted?"

"They were satisfactory at close quarters and new gun sight adjustments were made."

"This Commander Scott has caused an uproar over the years with his insistence upon gun drill and proper training. From what I've been told, he has been warned on a number of occasions to lay off or his promotion prospects could be damaged."

"I shouldn't think he would be scared off by that, sir. The man came across as being extremely dedicated where gunnery was concerned. Seemed to think the entire navy was very lacking on gun accuracy and told a few nightmarish stories to add weight to his belief."

"Really, like what?"

"He said that during the bombardment of the Alexandrian forts, three thousand shells were fired by eight battleships and only ten hits were recorded."

"Yes, that's common knowledge. Happened about sixteen years ago. The man is right to emphasise the importance of gunnery, but I think some clever sod put him with *Thunder Child* because they wanted him nicely out of the way. Now they want a ship that stands a chance of hitting one of these things and is expendable if it doesn't."

"And this old tub has, by sheer fluke, been in the right place at the wrong time, as far as we're concerned." Chudleigh realised what the Captain was getting at. "My word, she's the ideal expendable item. She's never been one for interest because she was a compromise between *HMS Captain* and *Devastation*."

"That's right," agreed Captain McIntosh. "I didn't even know she existed until four days ago. She's a closet ship, nicely tucked away doing mundane things."

"Right, sir, she's been totally neglected for twenty-five years and that's because *HMS Captain* met with disaster off Cape Finisterre. Within a year, Reed's *HMS Devastation* was launched and he wouldn't sanction anything linked to the *Captain*, except the turrets. The plans for this ship were already approved and building went ahead quite by accident, and somehow without Reed's knowledge until it was too late."

"So, Number One. *Thunder Child* has been a ship kept out of the way and officered by men who the navy wants out of the way, too. Am I right?" The captain came to the point, causing Chudleigh to smile.

"Yes, sir, you are right. *Thunder Child* is an out-of-the-way ship, officered by men who have been involved in some form of scandal."

Captain McIntosh shook his head in disbelief. "I wonder if I've done anything to upset them, or if I'm here on Scott's recommendation. They must have tried to offload him, but the man has made many powerful allies in Parliament and by complete mischance, his enemies have been given an expendable, obsolete, yet capable little ship to play with."

Chudleigh smiled and raised his glass. "Somehow I don't feel that privileged, Captain."

"No, Number One, I shouldn't think you do," he laughed and raised his glass too. "To *Thunder Child* and her outdated guns, and sod the bastards who are now evacuating the navy college for the oncoming Martians."

Following Mister Stanley's Example

They whimpered when the first fear of the darkness engulfed them, but Mister Stanley whispered words of encouragement to each of them, and gradually acceptance that the toxic gas outside the coal bunker couldn't get in became apparent. They had been in the bunker for over two hours, and the pandemonium outside had ended long ago in clamorous mass hysteria that each could only imagine in their dark solitude.

"Maybe it hasn't settled here," said the older sailor. "When should we go outside?"

"Perhaps it hasn't," agreed Mister Stanley. "But I would advise you to stay here and keep the coal and handkerchief to your mouth and continue breathing through it. The train driver at Woking swore by it, and I survived because I was inside the wrecked train carriage. Therefore, I must conclude that both methods would give us a better chance."

"The panic outside is gone, and I can't hear that thing either," Mrs Wade trembled fearfully, yet also with anger.

"I'm afraid to say, Mrs Wade that I fear everyone outside will have been killed by the toxic smoke or the light beam." His words were sullen, but precise.

"How can you be so sure, Mister Stanley?" Her distressed voice came out of the darkness.

He reached out and took her hand, giving it a gentle squeeze. "I've seen the devastation before, and what we must do is get out to sea in the small boat you have in the yard when night comes. No doubt, one of the passing sea vessels will pick us up. There are so many of them out there, we can't be missed."

"We'll need a lantern," added the older sailor. "Or we'd be chopped up at night. I don't see why we should wait until darkness."

"I think it would be prudent."

"I can't believe its happening."

The younger sailor's voice was full of apprehension. "I keep pinching myself. I keep expecting to wake up in my bed and see this same blackness."

Within their compact void, there was silent agreement with the young man; he felt as though he could see them nodding their heads.

"It would be so nice if that were the case," said Mrs Wade kindly.

"Aye," added the older sailor. "It would be total bliss."

"Do you think I should strike a match?" asked the young sailor. "I want to know the time."

"No lights," cut in Mister Stanley. "The train driver at Woking said the cloud could have some form of methane in it. We can't take the chance, especially sitting on this coal."

"The machine-creature fires its light through the smoke. It causes explosions, but the black cloud doesn't ignite." The older sailor was offering something of his own logic.

"Yes," agreed Mister Stanley, having second thoughts. "You are right. The creature did fire its light through the smoke and there were explosions within. It might be worth the risk."

"I've got matches," said the youngster.

Mister Stanley pulled his pocket watch out of his waistcoat. "And I have the time, let's strike a match, lad."

The welcoming flash lit up the cramped bunker and all flinched before the intense brightness as their pupils dilated adequately to accommodate the new light.

Every face was covered in soot, and there was an almost comical aspect to each person as they stared at one another nervously. In other circumstances, they might have started giggling, but the forbidding world beyond their dark lair was engulfing their sanctimonious refuge.

"It's five-fifteen, we dare not leave yet," Mister Stanley advised.

"That thing might be standing there," added the youngster.

"I think it's moved on," added the old sailor

"Let's wait a bit longer." Mrs Wade sounded agitated and nervous. She also felt the older sailor was too challenging of Mister Stanley, who seemed like a very important man.

The younger sailor yelped as his match burned out and plunged them, once again, into darkness.

"If it has moved on, we could be wasting valuable time." The older sailor was becoming restless and it had begun to manifest all of a sudden. They had been sent from their ship to accompany Mister Stanley into Herne Bay, while he tried to see if there were any land-based telegrams sent from London. There was nothing, and then they had complied with instructions to set up a coastal link with the Reculver Abbey semaphore. This had all been done and he was unsure of Mister Stanley's standing, even though he was from the War Office. "I think one of us should venture out." There was a hint of defiance in his voice.

"I would earnestly advise you not to. Wait until nightfall, then we can make our way around the side of Mrs Wade's cottage with the boat and go straight down to the sea."

"I disagree. We should leave as soon as possible." The old sailor was defiant.

"If you wish to go out and explore while we remain here, then do so." Mister Stanley remained calm but focused his argument directly at the old seaman. "You take the risks if you want to."

There was a brief silence before the reply came.

"Right then. I'll do that." There was an air of defiance in the seaman's voice.

Gingerly, he opened the lid and shafts of daylight pierced the blackness. Not blue like the summer day earlier before the Martian came, but grey with an eerie fog. He slid out and fell to the yard floor, still clutching the handkerchief to his mouth, while behind him, the coal bunker lid closed. Slowly, he sat up and for a moment, as he peered through the grey mist wondering why it had changed colour—no longer being black—it looked less harmful. Perhaps it had diluted and was no longer toxic. There was no feeling of giddiness or nausea, though he still clutched the coal-filled hankie to his mouth.

Slowly, he stood up and looked about the yard and, perceiving the kitchen door, began to creep towards it. The mist seemed to part invitingly for him as he moved forward towards the cottage. Upon reaching the backdoor, he stopped to peer back at the coal bunker from where he had emerged. It looked snug, nestled in the fog. His gaze wandered beyond to the yard wall and up to the thicker grey haze beyond the yard perimeter. It began to break down and he could make out a ribbed pole comprised of a strange dirty white alloy in the thinning dimness. Too thick for a flag pole and then his heart skipped a beat when he saw the vein-like pipe running up the side. The fog parted some more and his glance raised as the vapour fell away to portray a distant trunk that towered above him.

He thought his heart had leapt up to lodge in his throat because he was terrified to the point of wanting to scream, but nothing would come out. Nothing but a pathetic and stifled gurgle as his knees started to quiver uncontrollably.

The enormous titan tilted downwards upon its legs with a sound of heavy grating alloy as its head trunk displayed the compound orbs that glowed out of the obscurity to stare down at his insect form. He froze! There was nothing he could do, for fear paralysed every muscle and fibre of his wretched form, apart from the spasms in his knees. His eyes were the only things that moved with proper control and they looked back longingly at the sanctuary of the bunker, where he could see Mister Stanley staring at him through the small opening of the slightly raised lid.

A tear came to the sorry seaman's eyes and Mister Stanley closed the top, just before a tentacle shot down and wrapped itself around the wretched seaman.

His scream finally came as he was lifted into the sky at great speed to fade away into the devouring grey eternity. Meanwhile, the three remaining survivors cringed in their dark abode—terror being their only host—as each beseeched God that their sanctity would not be betrayed. For ages, they shivered in dreadful anticipation, expecting the lid to be lifted to display the horrendous monstrosity that eagerly awaited them. Time passed and nothing happened. They huddled together in the darkness and continued to wait, gathering courage before they would strike their next match to see the time—waiting for an eternity before they would even dare to talk.

CHAPTER 7

THE QUARTERMASTER'S BETTER SIDE

Perry was inside the fore turret with the gun crew—listening carefully as Fancourt explained how the recoil cylinders worked, being served by the recoil exhaust water tank. He was fascinated by the engineering of it all, and found it hard to believe these particular guns were obsolete and, as far as they knew, the neglected *Thunder Child* was the only vessel in the Royal Navy with muzzle-loading guns.

"Now your guns slide back along the cylinders here so as we can tilt the muzzles down." The gun crew pulled the two iron monsters back so the muzzles came inside the turret, where two iron pendulums swung down to close the vacant gun ports. "Now if you look down, you'll see the hydraulic loading rams. Two for charges and two for shells."

"I've seen the rams below deck, near the mess," added Perry.

"That's right, lad. They likes to keep stacks of shells there when they're firing and things can get a bit crowded when that happens."

They tilted the guns to give Perry a demonstration of what the process involved, placing them over the hydraulic loaders where the charges came up.

"Now when firing, we must always check the barrel before reloading. Do you know why?" began Fancourt.

"To make sure the shell 'as fired," replied Perry.

"That's right, boy. There was a terrible accident in Gibraltar with one of these things about twenty years ago."

"When they were still obsolete," added one of the other gun crew jokingly.

Fancourt turned and smiled. "All right, all right, we all know they went out with the square wheel." He then came back to Perry. "These men fired both guns at the same time and covered their ears so as not to be deafened by the roar. They do make one awful boom that goes clean through you. Well, when they went back to the guns after, no one looked into the barrels and what they didn't know was that only one gun had gone off. The other still had a shell and charge inside it. So when they went back to the hydraulic rams, another charge and shell was placed on top of the first one. When the guns were fired again, the jammed barrel blew up killing the men inside the turret. An explosion like that in a confined space is deadly, as I'm sure you can well imagine."

At that moment, Quartermaster Middleton entered the turret and smiled to the old gunner. "How's Boy First Class Perry making out, Gunner Fancourt?"

"He's got the potential to be a good seaman, Quartermaster Middleton."

"Does he now?" The Middleton trademark was in full bloom, but this time, Perry found the man less menacing. "Well, young Perry, I thought once you've had a look around here, we might go down to the stokehold and engine rooms."

"Yes, Quartermaster," agreed Perry with an enthusiasm, which was noted. He was enjoying what Fancourt had told him and was equally as keen to see the stokehold.

"Well now, I can accommodate you there, young man. It would be a good thing to assess such potential and see what you're made of, lad. It's up to you to take things seriously and aim for the type of work you think you're cut out for. Do you have ambition, Perry?"

"Yes, Quartermaster, I do."

"Right then, lad. That's good and it's up to the Royal Navy to take advantage of such zeal and you to use that purpose. We're trading with the navy you see, boy."

He looked up at Gunner Fancourt. "Have you finished with the lad, Gunner?"

"I have indeed, Quartermaster. He's all yours."

"Splendid," he beamed. "Come along then, lad, let's show you the ship you'll trade with. She wants the best from you, and you must make sure you can get the very best from her."

"Yes, Quartermaster." Perry's ambition was being fuelled as Middleton built the young man's confidence with the pride of his beloved country.

"We live in illustrious times, young Perry, and I think this nation is probably at its peak of greatness. These are the times you were born into, young man, and you've wisely joined the supreme tool of Empire in Her Majesty's Navy."

Perry was totally sucked in by Middleton's lecture, listening intently as they went along the main deck's guardrail. They passed the wheelhouse and continued to a hatchway further down, where a ladder descended past the main deck, close to the aft gun loading rams and lower to the middle deck, where his own sleeping area was amidships. Aft went to the captain's cabin. The engine room was below, still amidships and occupying a large area so that the aft lower deck came to a halt at the rear part of the wall. They came down onto a grilled platform suspended above the engineering section.

Perry had known it was here, but had never ventured down until now. A small stairway took them to the starboard engine, where huge pipes were on either side of them, driving the starboard propeller. The hum and vibration of turning machinery surrounded them, and Middleton raised his voice to be heard.

"This is where it all happens, Perry." He swung a hand out. Engineers were walking about checking and monitoring things, looking the picture of efficiency. "That man there, standing before the telegraph order receiver, is working the main engine throttle from the reading he just got. From that, he can read the speed required in the bridge."

"Is that what Lieutenant Faulbs calls down through the voice pipe, Quartermaster?" Perry was trying to put together the chain of command.

"It is, lad, but his orders go to the helmsman. You've seen him, haven't you?"

"Yes, Quartermaster."

"Well the two crewmen standing before him are telegraph men. One for starboard, the other for…" He lingered, wanting Perry to complete the rest.

"Port." The youngster was listening intently.

"These men send down the orders being read on the telegraph…" Again, he waited.

"Order receiver," completed Perry.

"Everywhere you go on board the ship, you'll see men like this. Good crewmen that make their contribution to the ship's running. You'll become one of these men, young Perry. Somewhere on this vessel, you'll find your place and we'll look upon you as reliable. We will depend on you and you, young man, will be proud of that trust."

"Yes, Quartermaster." Perry so wanted to be trusted and accepted. Middleton was doing an excellent job. He could not help but begin to trust the quartermaster. There was much more to this man then a harsh manner. He took young seamen seriously and wanted them trustworthy.

"That's right, young Perry. I mean you." It was as though he had read the youngster's thoughts. "You can make the grade. You will make the grade, but in what area?" He turned and led the way to the rails near the starboard hull and as they looked forward, another set of stairs led down to the stokehold.

Perry felt the intense heat and wondered how the men could work in such conditions. He counted four stokes, each with four hatches, where stokers opened one while another quickly shovelled coal that was piled against the hull's curve, into the furnace. He was looking down on the men from the gantry, by the engineering section, and thought the heat in front of the stoke furnaces must be unbearable. The stokers laboured on—stripped to the waist and covered in black dust. They toiled and sweated with their efforts to keep the ship in motion.

"Sorts the men out from the boys, aye, lad?" Middleton looked down at the stokehold. "Not for me, I'll admit, and somehow I don't think it's what you would want either."

"No, Quartermaster," he agreed.

"Now what about a signalman, young Perry? You're literate and you learn quickly."

His eyes widened and Middleton knew he had a flicker of interest from the young man.

"Well now," he smiled. This was within the quartermaster's realm and it pleased him. "Come along then, Perry, and let's take you to the semaphore. We'll see what you're made of and I'll put you alongside the signalman for a couple of days and see how you make out."

Before leaving, Perry spared a last sympathetic glance back at the stokehold as the men toiled by the furnaces. To him, it was a vision of hell and he felt relief he was not a stoker. These men were forged from a special type of metal, one he was happy not to be cast from. They went back up the ladder way through the various decks until emerging from the superstructure close to the aft turret. After the heat of the stokehold, the chill sea breeze hit them, especially Perry, who felt the contrast strongly. A ladder was connected to the rear of the aft turret and he followed Middleton up so they both stood on top of the circular armoured gun casing. A set of steps led down from the aft deck of the superstructure and stopped at about a foot above the revolving turret.

"Up you go then, lad." The quartermaster was enjoying the walk about and it was ending at a task where his responsibilities were concerned.

Perry complied and came out on the superstructure's aft part of the deck, where lifeboats hung from gantries on either side and in front was the mast. Beyond the two funnels, which led down to the recently departed stoke room, spewed out black smoke as the sturdy ironclad ploughed through the sea. He looked below to the stern, where beyond, above the ship's wake, seagulls flew just above the white bilge. The quartermaster stood beside him and looked to starboard. The array of different vessels was astonishing. Battleships from Britain, France and Germany cruised along with yachts, smacks and paddle steamers—a vast exodus—all moving northwards along the Kent coastline.

They proceeded along the portside until reaching the semaphore platform, where a signalman was standing by a post with his arms hanging idle for the moment.

"That's one instrument of communication but, as you know, we also use lights and flags," Middleton began to explain. He called to the signalman at the end of the platform and explained why he had Boy First Class Perry with him. The signalman exchanged words of confirmation, and nodded with a smile. "Right, lad, you wait here while I go and see the captain. You'll be running backwards and forwards with messages if he allows you to stay with the signalmen."

He went into the bridge, where Perry made out the forms of Captain McIntosh and the French liaison officer as the quartermaster opened the hatch.

Once he was alone, he looked back to the signalman, who was watching the shoreline. There was another on the starboard side watching the other vessels—an ordinary seaman stood at the end of his platform and Perry wondered if he was a potential signals learner as well. He began to think of his rank if he progressed. Signalman Perry, Chief Signalman Perry and who knew, maybe even Quartermaster Perry one day. He looked out at the array of ships and marvelled at the sight. His first voyage and during such an historic event. Into battle stations straight away with a real chance of seeing action. Action. The word froze in his mind and then dread began to kick in. They were going to fight Martian tripods no one had seen or could even begin to imagine. He wondered if he would be reliable when confronted by such monstrosities. He thought of the stokehold beneath the water line and what it would be like to be down in such a place if the vessel was sinking. It was hard to imagine the possibility when standing on the superstructure looking out above the waves, but all too real in the enclosed confines of the stokehold.

The signalman on the starboard side relayed a message to the ordinary seaman, who at once marched to the bridge. Perry couldn't help but be inquisitive as to what was happening. This wasn't a message from a shoreline battery—the signalman was facing seaward—and must have taken some notation from another vessel. He wandered over to the starboard side, his interest getting the better of him. Before he could try to make out what was happening amid the many ships, Quartermaster Middleton came out of the bridge. He walked up to him with a smile on his face and said. "Well then, young Perry, you might want to run back to your quarters and get something thicker to wear. You'll be with the port signalman and you'll be running messages in and out of the bridge when necessary."

"Yes, Quartermaster," he replied and sped off to the conning tower and went down through the steering position. He made a point of coming out the starboard side of the main deck, hoping to see what had caught the signalman's attention amid the international exhibition of fine shipping.

A large German vessel was coming through the flotilla, the ship moving in a different direction from every other craft. She was resplendent, flying the flag of Germany from her main mast.

Gunner Fancourt came walking along the guardrail from the fore turret. He was smiling at Perry's open-mouthed surprise. It was obvious the youngster had a love of ships and was mesmerised by the new foreign vessel on a rendezvous course with *Thunder Child.*

"Blimey, who's she?" he asked the old gunner.

"That's *Konig Wilhelm.* Had a bit of tarting up, she 'as too. No more masts and rigging."

"Are the Germans going to muck in too then?"

"As far as I know, every nation that can get here will send ships."

Perry shook his head in pleasurable disbelief. "With all this lot growing bigger by the minute, we'll have enough clout to give the Martians a bit to think about."

He walked to the rear of the gun deck and stopped at the next hatchway, where a second ladder went down to his quarters on the main deck.

Behind, Gunner Fancourt laughed as Perry hastened down, muttering. "Young Perry might have found his place already."

The Patience of Mister Stanley

"I think it will have to be me who goes out first," said the young sailor nervously in the confining gloom.

He was trying hard to be courageous, but he was terrified.

"If anything happens to you, Mister Stanley, it'll be difficult for Mrs Wade and myself."

"It'll be difficult for all of us whatever happens, lad."

Mister Stanley's ever-consoling voice was the one soothing thing the darkness thankfully contained. "It is my earnest ambition to get us all out of this mess. I intend to do it and, by God, it will happen. Strike another match, lad, and I'll see what the time is."

The young sailor fumbled in the darkness for a moment, then suddenly there was a welcome flash that once again caused them to blink while they adjusted to the light. Mister Stanley was quick to look at his watch.

"Five past seven," he muttered. "God, its June and we still have at least two hours of daylight."

"I'll go out carefully and stand against the backyard wall," offered the young sailor again. "I'll open the backyard door just a wee bit to look."

"It's too risky, boy. Not yet, let's wait a little longer." Mrs Wade was fighting a battle of containment. Her voice was shaky and the strain was beginning to tell.

Mister Stanley took a deep breath as the match light went out. "Well, we can't continue like this. I'll go."

There followed immediate protests from Mrs Wade and the young sailor. Mister Stanley raised his arm for silence. It was a pointless thing to do as none could see in the pitch darkness.

"I'll be extremely cautious and will make straight for the wall, which this bunker is against. I don't know why, but I think the creature was on the other side of the wall."

"It might see you," protested Mrs Wade.

Again, Mister Stanley reached out and touched the frightened lady's hand. "Mrs Wade, we must attempt something sooner or later and we need to know the lay of the land. I'll be as watchful as I can. I promise you."

He gingerly pushed up the lid a fraction and peeped out into the yard. The mist was all but gone, and the clear day was once again in place. It was deathly quiet, however, and the absence of seagulls was notable. It left an uncanny impression upon the little world of Mrs Wade's backyard.

Cautiously, he raised the top further and gingerly climbed out, closing the lid once his feet were firmly on the ground. For a moment, he waited while gathering his frightened wits and regulating his breathing so that he calmed. Climbing out of the coal bunker had been a major feat—more so than he imagined it to be. After a while, he began to look cautiously about him. The evening was clear and the recent foul-smelling mist had cleared. At any other time, it would have been a wonderful, late-summer evening. All he could hear was the sound of the sea, almost haunting as it splashed upon the distant and unseen shingle at the front of the cottage. Satisfied there was nothing immediately in sight, he darted towards the yard wall and pressed himself against it. He began regulating his breathing, taking clear, precise breaths in an effort to slow his wildly thumping heart. God! He was frightened and it took every ounce of his will to overcome the dreadful fear that spread throughout his body. He began to shake and sweat profusely, and he tried desperately to control himself. The image of the older sailor's horrendous death came back to him briefly, but he forced it from his mind and slowly made his way towards the backyard door where he quickly and gently lifted the latch before pulling it ajar—just enough to peer up the steep slope.

The sight before him was horrendous as he stared in terror at the scattered and blackened corpses that lay everywhere. He was about to slam the loathsome sight from view, but managed, yet again, to overcome the temptation, for there were no tripods in view. To the east, he could hear the distant scream of the Martians, but it was some distance off, perhaps in Margate. He looked back at the multitude of dead that lay covered in black soot and twisted in their agonised death throws, as though rigor mortis had appeared suddenly and complete.

Pulling the door wider, he went through and carefully closed it behind him. His heartbeat was beginning to settle, despite the devastation all about. With the fluttering in the pit of his stomach subsiding, on an instinct he walked up the slope towards the road that led out of Herne Bay. Picking his way through the scattered corpses, he reached the top and was overwhelmed by the slaughter on the road. The sight was terrible—many were cuddling each other, almost violently, in their agonised last moments. His eyes began to swell and a lump in his throat caused him to gag in an effort to contain the grief that began to ooze down his coal-encrusted cheeks.

There were families lying scattered about—dead children cuddling into parents, who had been desperately clinging to each other during their final agony—desperate for the one final thing they had left at the bitter end—their unyielding and undying love.

He turned his gaze to the blue sky as he shook his head in disbelief and gritted his teeth before God.

"You watched it all."

The anger went as quickly as it came, for it was fruitless. He now felt selfish, because he was relieved he had no children that would suffer this tribulation.

He reached the top of the slope and hung his head in despair, while before him, the hilltop road was littered with more clumped, slain humanity. He shook his head despondently and muttered.

"Good Lord! What do we do now? Where do we go from here?"

It was a beautiful day, with the dying sun shining over the green fields and the splashing tide. In the distance, masses of shipping continued to pass. Some of it away, northwards, other vessels turned westwards, along the coastline, heading towards the Thames estuary. All seemed oblivious to the death and destruction that was before him.

"Why not?" he argued with himself. *For what could be done?*

A sudden whimpering was heard upon the breeze—a child crying and in need of help. He looked about him anxiously and his gaze rested upon an old cart turned upon its side. A giant Shire horse lay dead beside it, and a few people were scattered close by—the owners, no doubt. The wailing was coming from under a canvas, towards which he approached with caution, but hoping above all that someone was alive. Gently, he lifted the material and saw a dead woman cuddling a bundle wrapped in a sheet. The lady's mouth was blackened and he guessed the wretched woman must have crawled under the canvas as the black smoke was taking everyone and in her last moment, got the precious gathering to the safety of the canvas.

He bent down and tenderly unwrapped the quivering bundle, to find a little girl of between eighteen months and two years. Her little whimpers touched his heart, and he experienced a kindling of joy that began to combat the anguish that had been overwhelming him.

Gently, he brushed back her long, matted auburn hair to reveal a soft, fair face with chubby cheeks that glistened from continuous sobbing. She was obviously afraid, and reluctant to leave the sanctuary of her dead mother's arms.

"Come on now, pet," whispered Mister Stanley soothingly. "I know a kind lady who will help you."

She looked up at him, still snivelling and sulking as though he might bring her dead mother back if she continued long enough.

"What's your name? Can you tell me that?" he asked tenderly.

The sobbing suddenly stopped as her large, brown eyes drank him in. She pursed her lips sadly, the way infants do when they realise they can't have what they would like but are still willing to take what is on offer. Rubbing her wet eyes while pondering, she took the plunge and held up her arms, accepting him as the next best thing.

"Good girl, come on now, let's get back to Mrs Wade."

He lifted her as she cuddled into him, shaking with the trauma she had been through. Quickly, he made his way down the slope and back to Mrs Wade's backyard.

He wasted no time once back, pulling the lid up to see Mrs Wade and the sailor blinking before the sunlight.

"Quick as you can now, the coast is clear. Mrs Wade, would you take the little girl for me please?"

"Oh my word," she replied, taking the infant, who seemed willing to be held by the kindly lady. "You poor little darling."

Mister Stanley looked at the young sailor. "You and me, lad, shall take the boat around the side of the cottage and down onto the beach. Mrs Wade, I would like you to go through the house and come out the front door and join us on the beach. I don't want you to go out the backdoor with us because there's a most terrible sight upon the hill."

Mrs Wade nodded her head and said. "Very well, Mister Stanley."

"Right," he began as he and the sailor took the small rowing boat and struggled towards the yard door.

"We're all getting out of here now and by sea."

CHAPTER 8
ACTIVITY AND SPECULATION

Captain McIntosh was watching from the bridge when the young ordinary seaman came inside to inform him of the sighting.

"*Konig Wilhelm's* signals, sir," he saluted and passed the message to Chudleigh. He handed it to the Captain and the young sailor left to return to the signalman on the starboard semaphore.

The officer of the watch went to the fore. He raised his binoculars and focused on the German battleship amid the fleet and the rest of the shipping off the starboard bow.

"Dropping way to come abeam. Incline of forty degrees at green twenty, sir."

All eyes focused upon the German vessel as her funnels spewed out smoke with the rest, though suddenly becoming distinct amid the other ships.

"Well, I think she looks better for her refit, sir," Chudleigh commented.

"Yes, she does," agreed the captain. "See to it that the men are ready to receive our guest, Number One."

"Very good, sir. Will you want him in the waiting room straight away?"

"As soon as possible."

Chudleigh went to the hatchway and saw Quartermaster Middleton waiting with the port signalman. He smiled as he went by, saying, "More guests coming aboard, Middleton. Hope the helmsman's good."

It was a light-hearted joke. Commander Chudleigh had good faith in all the steersmen, but it amused him to say such things because Middleton, ever conscientious, would be down in the wheelhouse after such a remark—just to be on the safe side.

As expected, Middleton raised an eyebrow. "Oh, coming abeam are they, sir?" He went straight to the conning tower where the ladder way led to the steering position.

"Dropping way at green twenty a moment ago."

Chudleigh allowed him to go down the ladder first, then followed. The helmsman was receiving orders through the voice pipe and watching the steering compass, while the two telegraph men stood at their respective engine orders—one port, the other starboard. Middleton was beside him in an instant.

"Well now, Harling. Is all going well?"

"Yes, Quartermaster," he said with confidence and relayed instructions from the navigation officer to the engine orders. Middleton was pleased, Harling had been moulded by him and was now one of the best. He looked to the commander, with his pride bristling from head to toe.

Before Chudleigh could say anything, Boatswain Pickles came through the hatch from the main deck.

"Ah, the very man," he greeted him, allowing Middleton to bask in his glory.

"Thought I might be needed, sir. *Konig Wilhelm* is laying way off the starboard bow," reported Pickles efficiently.

Perry entered wearing a heavy-duty smock. He was on his way aloft to the portside semaphore and was taken aback by the ranks that seemed to be gathering in the wheelhouse. He stood to attention and saluted Chudleigh, who took no notice of him.

Middleton gave him a quick reassuring nod and said. "Off you go, lad, look sharp." In an instant,

Perry was gone—up the ladder and away to his new duty.

"Right then, Boatswain, let's get to it. Are your rope men ready?" Chudleigh was enjoying himself and was comfortable in the company of the quartermaster and boatswain.

"Ready and waiting, sir." Pickles was much like the quartermaster and between them, they held a secure grip over the crew. When he said things were done and ready, he meant it. Both were vital players in the ship's running.

As the *Konig Wilhelm* came abeam, the fore turret's gun crew peered out the gun ports, watching Pickles and Commander Chudleigh arrive at the scene. Their response to the German ship was a mixture of awe and resentment.

"She's looking fine, all right, and no doubt about that." Fancourt wasn't one for undermining things. "I've seen the old girl before, when she still had the old sail rigging."

"Built in one of our shipyards, though." The gun captain thought the ship was fine, too. It was British built.

"Not good seamen, though. She collided with one of her own and sunk it, killing five hundred crewmen." Hainscroft, another member of the gun crew, was more derogatory.

Fancourt looked at him. "What do you know about seamanship, you blooming greeny?"

The gun captain agreed. "We've made such mistakes ourselves, and more recently. These things are tragedies, Hainscroft, and it happens to seaman with years of experience."

Hainscroft went quiet—not wanting to argue with senior seamen. They watched as the vessels came abeam and began to draw closer. Rope men began working to establish a link between the two ships, and a young liaison lieutenant came along and stood with Chudleigh and Pickles.

"Who's the officer?" asked Hainscroft.

"Lieutenant Dyer," answered Fancourt. "Must speak German. He'll be our exchange man."

"Wonder what the German officer will be like in return." The gun captain frowned. "Never known a commotion like this—never in all my years. This is getting more eerie by the hour. This Martian affair is certainly causing a stir at sea. What must it be like on land?"

"God knows. I hear they're walking about in Surrey and Kent now and are on the outskirts of South London. People are running eastwards and soon the shoreline might be full of people—a mass exodus—as the population is routed." Fancourt was aware of the unfolding events, perhaps more so than others could grasp.

Hainscroft asked tentatively. "Don't you think it's the likes of us that might be panicking? Maybe we're getting information from the offshore signals and they're overreacting."

Fancourt shook his head. "No, boy. Mark my words, this is going to get worse before it gets better. Ever seen masses of people leaving their homes? I have in China. Saw it from a ship during a cholera epidemic. Hordes of people on the shoreline as far as the eye could see. No one would take them on board because it would spread throughout the ship. What's happening now will be worse than that. When the rush comes, and believe me it will, they'll be a sight of swarming humanity—the likes of which 'as never been seen before. They'll have to be lifted and I think, even with this array of shipping, we'll be hard pushed to do it."

"You're doom and gloom, Fancourt, but I hate to admit it…" The gun captain looked at Hainscroft bewildered. "He's usually right."

"For what it's worth, I hope I'm wrong on this occasion." He got up and looked through the gun port as the German liaison officer was welcomed aboard. He was a second lieutenant and stood proudly before Commander Chudleigh and saluted.

A strong breeze whipped up, sweeping along the starboard deck where Chudleigh returned the salute. "Herr Leutnant Hienmann, welcome aboard."

Hienmann smiled and replied. "It is an honour and privilege, Commander. Thank you."

Like Lieutenant Devour, his English was very good and he had a bright, approachable manner that oozed with enthusiasm. France and Germany had picked their liaison officers with great care.

"I'd like to escort you to the waiting room, Leutnant Hienmann, where the captain and some other officers will debrief you on the current state of affairs. I take it that you have heard what is going on."

"I know there is a meteorite that has landed in England and it has caused some kind of disaster."

Chudleigh frowned. "Is that all you've heard, Leutnant?"

"Yes, sir."

"Good God. Be prepared to be awestruck."

"What is the nature of this disaster, sir?" The German Leutnant zur See followed Chudleigh as he walked aft along the main deck. "We were getting signals from merchant vessels, but our captain would not disclose them. Our ship was alive with rumours, of course…" He laughed. "But these were a little too far-fetched. I believe that is the correct word."

Chudleigh stopped by the aft turret. "Far-fetched might be the correct word, Leutnant—I've a strange feeling you're going to relate rumours that are true."

Heinemann began to laugh quietly, but then his eyes widened when Chudleigh stared coldly back at him. The young German's face became bemused and a look of astonishment surfaced. "Not these tales of Martian tripods, Commander, surely not?"

"I think you should wait until the captain briefs you about our uncanny circumstance." Chudleigh went down the central ladder way onto the quarterdeck and into the hatchway behind. Heinemann was almost jogging along the companionway to keep up with the commander's long, purposeful strides. They descended to the middle deck and made their way aft.

Up on the superstructure, Perry stood by the portside semaphore at the start of the gantry. He watched the signalman jolt upright as he began scribbling on a pad.

"Write this down as well, can you?" the signalman said.

Perry fumbled for his pencil, then looked up, poised and ready.

"Martians advancing on London. City being evacuated. Death toll mounting. All forces sent to engage tripods have been smashed. Ashford, Kent under attack."

Perry wrote the signalman's words down and was then forced to read them back to make sure they were correct.

"Good, take them to the captain right away. There's no more yet, but get back as soon as you can." The signalman turned and watched the shoreline, leaving Perry to do his task.

He knocked upon the hatchway and entered, feeling it wasn't necessary to wait for a reply. All heads were turned to him as he entered, including Captain McIntosh, who was standing with Lieutenant Faulbs by the voice pipe. Taking two brisk paces towards the captain, he stopped and smartly saluted.

"Message from the port semaphore, sir," said Perry as the note was snatched and read quickly.

"Very good, Perry, dismissed," replied the Captain.

Complying, he turned, wanting to be away from the dismal bridge. So the Martians were as close as Ashford. They were spreading across the country like a putrid disease—a cancer no one could stop. He shivered at the thought of confronting such things, and his mind tried to build a picture of what they must look like. Try as he might, there was no way he could visualise them. He saw three great legs that went up into dull, grey mist, but the body was obscure. The thought vanished as he opened the door and stepped out onto the open deck once again. Above, the blue expanse and the sound of the green sea bathed his mind. The shoreline was dotted with people—lots of people—and for the first time, the tranquillity of the coastline was challenged. Before, it was hard to contemplate that there was anything wrong, but now it was different. The number of people who could be seen was too great, and the scene incited alarm. There were numerous clusters moving parallel with the shipping—not couples, but families—who carried possessions. Some had carts and many were waving as though desperate for ships to come towards the shore for them. It was a breach in a dam of composure—that first trickle of what would soon become an outpouring rush of uncontained humanity.

He reached the semaphore and the signalman noticed the look of concern on his face. "It's getting a bit too blooming close for comfort, isn't it, aye?"

"Christ, how long have they been there?"

"Just started, really. Well, I noticed a few more than usual, but it 'as just intensified since I got the signal. I think they're heading for Margate. They want to get out of the country."

Perry shook his head and sighed. "I can't see what good that will do. If these things fall from space, they can land in France as easy as they can land in Britain."

The signalman looked to shore again, nodding his head. "I make you right, but I don't think they have. All the foreign shipping seems to be heading this way. These things seem to be going about it in a systematic way. They must know something about us and the way we are."

"What, you mean they know we have borders?"

"They might do," the signalman said. "Then again, an island like ours would make a nice springboard for world conquest. They could sort themselves out properly and defend the shores before making their next move."

"Here we are with the most powerful navy the world 'as ever seen, and these Martians have rendered it useless. They don't cross the sea like our enemies from the past—they fall from the sky—making the sea a redundant place to put our defensive capabilities." Perry raised his eyebrow in a speculative manner.

The signalman grinned at him. "Blimey, you swallowed a flipping dictionary have you? Where do get to using words like that?"

"Why, what's wrong with them?" Perry smiled, pleased he was of amusement to the signalman.

"Nothing's wrong with them at all, if you want to talk like an upper-crust officer an' all. They're the sort of words they use."

They relaxed and got to know one another as the summer evening wore on. They kept watch of the shoreline and chatted about mundane things. Where they were from, and what they would do when their navy days were done, while steady throngs of people along the shoreline became more numerous as they progressed northward, towards the Thames estuary.

Mister Stanley Stops a Paddle Steamer

"Ahoy there," shouted Mister Stanley and Lawrence as they stood up in the old rowing boat, waving their arms very nervously against the craft's progressive rolling.

"I think they have seen us," added Mrs Wade as she cuddled the young infant with one arm and grabbed the boat's side with the other. "I think it would be prudent to sit down now," she added, becoming somewhat tense at the small vessel's severe rolling.

Sensing Mrs Wade's growing anxiety, Lawrence grasped Mister Stanley to stop him falling over the side. "I'm sure they've seen us," he added as they both gingerly sat down.

"Thank God for that," added Mister Stanley. "I was beginning to worry that it might get dark with us drifting into the shipping lanes."

"It's a paddle steamer," added the young sailor as the welcome sight of the vessel pulled away from the shipping traffic and made towards them—its long and narrow tan-coloured funnel spewed smoke into the gathering dusk. Its bow and keel were black up to the bulwarks where, from there on, the cabin area was white. As the paddle steamer chugged closer, they made out the name along the bow.

"*The Southend Belle*," uttered Mister Stanley. "It's one of those day-tripper boats that go from the pier of Southend, over the Essex side. What's it doing out this far?"

"It's not unusual, Mister Stanley," added Mrs Wade. "Many of the boats come out this far during the summertime."

The appreciated advance of the paddleboat brought about an infectious joy that inundated all as it came alongside them and its engine clinked out of gear. Even the tiny infant sensed the situation was good and her eyes widened as she pointed at the paddle steamer.

"Yes, darling," replied Mrs Wade, giving the little girl a reassuring hug. "They are coming for us."

The great paddle wheels suddenly stopped, leaving the vessel to drift and make way alongside their small rowing boat. Crewmen came to the port bow and threw down a rope.

"Thank you," called Mister Stanley, while Lawrence grabbed the line.

"Let yourself drift amidships, beyond the paddle wheel casing. There's a hatchway there," shouted a crewmember.

They complied as the small rowing boat fell along the drifting paddle steamers portside—watching excitedly as the white grids of the paddle wheel casing floated gently by. As the hatchway came upon them, another crewman threw a second rope, which was eagerly gathered up. Within minutes, all four of them were aboard *The Southend Belle*, having been quickly lifted through the side hatchway. The little rowing boat was left to drift in the coming dusk.

"Thank you," said Mister Stanley.

"My pleasure, sir," replied an older member of the crew. He turned to Lawrence and smiled. "Some of your Royal Navy boys are on board."

Lawrence just smiled. "Well, I'm glad to hear that, sir."

"Yes, we lost one of the shore party in Herne Bay," added Mister Stanley. "The town has been attacked by a Martian tripod thing. It's killed hundreds."

"You've seen one, then." The older sailor looked bemused—almost disbelieving.

"Yes we have," Mrs Wade trembled angrily. "This poor little mite lost her parents and now we're all she has. If it weren't for Mister Stanley, who bravely went out and searched the area, she would have been left amid the carnage, all alone fending for herself."

Mister Stanley looked embarrassed at the praise when Lawrence spoke up.

"It's true! If it wasn't for Mister Stanley, I don't know what we would be doing now. Thank you, sir."

The young sailor held out his hand to him. "I think this crisis 'as brought out something special in you, if you don't mind me saying so, sir."

Mister Stanley smiled and shook Lawrence's hand. He decided the praise was gratifying and given sincerely by both, and he was grateful to them. He was learning much about himself, and how wonderful other people were. It suddenly occurred to him that he had never tried to get to know anyone before the terrible dilemma of the Martian invasion had happened. He had been a mother's boy who worked for the government. It was as though he had never been born until the train crash at Woking station.

"Well, I'm glad there's something good coming out of all this mess," added the old seaman of the paddle steamer. "We're on our way to the pier at Southend. The place is full of refugees and we've been ordered to ferry people to Ostend in Belgium."

"I see," replied Mister Stanley, looking at Mrs Wade and the infant.

"You can go there too," added the old seaman reassuringly. "But we'll obviously need to get to the pier first.

"That's very kind." He looked to Mrs Wade and smiled. "Right now, I think this is our best course of action."

"Are there no Martians in Belgium then?" asked Mrs Wade bemused.

"Apparently not yet, madam, but we can't be totally sure. It seems people are trying to flee to countries like Belgium, France and Holland, so we assume the Martians aren't there yet."

"Yet, being the operative word." Mister Stanley scratched his jaw perplexed. "These things can drop anywhere upon the entire planet. Why would they only land in Britain?"

The old seaman smiled. "I can't rightly give you a definite answer, Mister Stanley, 'cause none of us rightly know. We're assuming."

He smiled politely at the man. "Well, I think I'll go up and sit on the open deck if I'm not needed anymore." He looked to Mrs Wade. "Would you join me?"

She nodded and smiled as she cuddled the little girl in her charge. "Of course we will."

He turned once more to O.S. Lawrence. "Goodbye and good luck."

"And the same to you, Mister Stanley." He left with one of the steamer's crew to be reunited with fellow Royal Navy men aboard the vessel.

"I'll have some cocoa sent aft if you're on the open deck, sir, and I reckon a blanket if you plan on staying up there for a while," added the old seaman.

"Thank you," replied Mister Stanley. "You are most kind."

"My pleasure, sir."

The old seaman left, while a younger crewman showed them aft to the open deck, where there were neat rows of empty benches. At this point, he left them too, though with a promise to attend to the matter of cocoa and blankets.

"Oh, look at this," said Mrs Wade to the little girl, who was cuddling into her firmly. "Look at all those stars in the sky."

To her surprise, the little girl looked up and pointed. It was the first positive response they had got from her.

"What's your name?" asked Mister Stanley kindly.

For a moment, the little girl looked at him as though deciding. Then she muttered something that he, nor Mrs Wade, could quite understand.

"Ooh really!" he replied. "That sounds nice. Could you say that again?"

"Jojo," she repeated a little more clearly.

"What a lovely name, my little petal," added Mrs Wade.

"No Jojo betal," added the little girl. "Jojo jo Neil."

"Jojo O'Neil," added Mister Stanley with a smile. "Yeah."

Her little head nodded and a smile creased her wonderful little face. They sat upon the bench and looked up at the clear night sky. The landward horizon to the southeast was falling away from them, and with it the flickering stretch of red radiance—an ominous aura from where Margate would be. However, it was far off and they tried to focus little Jojo's attention on the night sky ahead of them, even managing to ignore the shooting star that shot across in a downward arc towards the west—the direction *The Southend Belle* was heading.

"You know," said Mister Stanley gently. "I'm not the person I was a day ago."

Mrs Wade looked to him, and smiled. He looked dishevelled, bald with spectacles, yet he retained a confidence about him that was manly in her view. She couldn't imagine him being any other way, and regarded him as a person used to giving orders. Not a bully, but more of an inspiring person who could lead by example.

"I'm sure all this is something that would change the best of us, Mister Stanley. I'm just glad you came along when you did. You were a miracle that came out of the terror and confusion."

He looked to her and smiled. Was that how she really visualised him? Quiet Albert Stanley, who had until so recently lived with his now departed mother—his mother's boy who worked for the Government at the War Office. Perhaps he would do better by not telling her things in such a way. Mrs Wade wanted someone strong and resourceful and if he'd gained anything from the Martian invasion, it was his self-esteem and knowledge that there were other things about him. The aptitude to telegram back to the War Office and the ability to try and comply with their instructions for offshore signal stations along the south coast. He probably wasn't the only person doing such things, but now he was moving about well amid the chaos.

He put his hand in hers and squeezed it reassuringly—a liberty he would never normally dared to take with a lady, but he was feeling bold and confident and he wanted Mrs Wade to feel his protective desire. It was important he convey his determination to see that she and Jojo would get through whatever might occur.

"Thank you, Mrs Wade. You have a most kind way with words." He smiled at her and looked into her soft brown eyes.

"When we go to Belgium, you won't leave us, will you, Mister Stanley?"

"No. I will not, that I promise."

She put her hand upon his neck and pulled him forward, whereupon she planted a gentle kiss on his cheek.

His chest swelled with pride and a stirring flowered within him. He realised he had developed a great affection for Mrs Wade, even though he had known her for only a few hours. He felt as though he would never want to leave her again and until he had met her, he had never really been born.

"Who knows what tomorrow may bring?" she said. "I do have a certain faith in you though, Mister Stanley—you seem like a survivor."

"Please, call me Albert." It was a kind request.

"If you will call me Daisy," came her girlishly shy reply.

They both sighed and sat back with little Jojo looking from one to the other with bemused and innocent eyes. The summer night's breeze fluttered their fringes as the paddle steamer went up the Thames estuary.

"We should be able to see the pier lights soon. When we pass Whitstable," said Daisy.

Behind them, a hatchway opened and the young crewman came out with a tray of mugs with sandwiches and biscuits.

"Here we go," he said enthusiastically. "I'll go back and get the blanket for you."

Behind and in the distance could be heard the sound of faraway cannons, but none heeded it. For the moment, they were safe.

CHAPTER 9
RED HORIZON

C aptain McIntosh looked out portside as he stood upon the open bridge. *Thunder Child* was nearing the Thames estuary and the spectacle of the refugees had gripped him. He found the engulfing night irritating because he could no longer make them out as clearly as before. There were still lights from dwellings, but these were mere dots that could illuminate nothing. Looking down at the white painted rivets of the ship's steel panelling, his mind drifted as a cool sea breeze swirled about him.

Chudleigh watched, knowing the captain would soon talk when his pondering was done. He could sense the man's mind ticking over, wondering no doubt, like himself, about the Martian advance— trying to visualise the way these extra-terrestrial creatures must look and how long it would be before they had the grim fortune of meeting the tripod fighting machines.

The door opened and Quartermaster Middleton came onto the open bridge—a severe expression on his face.

"Next station making way at red twenty, sir," he said to Chudleigh, sensing the captain might not want to be disturbed.

McIntosh sighed and brought his binoculars to bear as the lights began to flicker. Middleton had pen and pad at the ready and began jotting down as the light began flicking its message.

23:15. London being evacuated. Martians in southwest suburbs and others in Kent. Troops deployed at Maidstone. Have engaged tripods. Many casualties. One tripod destroyed by artillery. Fierce fighting at Canterbury. Cathedral in flames. Archbishop and many townspeople killed.

"Again it's repeating the message," said Chudleigh. "I wonder how long it'll be before they get their next news."

"I don't think it'll be too long, sir. The station will be in sight for a little while longer yet. "

"Yes," agreed the captain. "This message is just five minutes old. The fighting's happening now."

"New ones, sir," called Middleton excited. "I hope they plugged another one of them."

Instantly, they focused back on the shore station with binoculars, hungry for more news and hoping to God for something positive.

23:25. Martians established in southwest London. Maidstone fallen. Canterbury fallen. Martians advancing eastward. Nothing to stop them in Kent. Parliament evacuated. Government placed in Edinburgh.

"Looks as though England is out of the equation," muttered Chudleigh.

"It'll not be long before they get to Scotland, too," added McIntosh. "Not at the rate they're advancing."

At that moment, Faulbs came to the hatch and called. "Signalman wants you to go to the semaphore, sir."

"It's all right, Faulbs, we can read the signals from here."

"It's not to do with the signals, Captain. The young lad assisting at the semaphore spotted a glow at red one forty. You'll get a better view aft, where they are."

The captain was mystified, and it showed in his glance to Middleton with raised eyebrow. "The young fledgling you've been showing the ropes to, Quartermaster?"

"Yes, sir. Boy Seaman Perry."

"Well," began Chudleigh. "The young chap seems excited about something."

They all went inside and made for the rear hatch that led onto the superstructure. Perry called excitedly as they emerged.

"There's something on the horizon over there, sir." He began gesturing excitedly across the port quarterdeck, where the land lay hidden in the blackness. A fresh breeze swept the deck and the smell of land rimmed the captain's nostrils. He couldn't be sure, maybe it was his imagination, but could he smell smoke too?

"You can just make it out, sir," added the signalman, who Perry was assisting. "He must have good eyesight to spot it."

As they neared the semaphore, the captain made out a red tinge along the distant and dark hinterland. An orange shade bathed the night sky—the result of distant fires. They were leaving the glow as *Thunder Child* carved a path through the black sea, putting distance between herself and the onshore fires.

"I want to take a closer look," the captain said. "Blast, we're moving away from it." He was tempted to turn the ship around, but stopped short of the action. His orders were decisive and he had to see them through. Quickly, he raised his binoculars and focused on the distant radiance, bathing the night sky where it rolled past the land's edge. Adjusting the focus, he made out the line of the land with hell in the background. Waves of red, orange and yellow rising and merging into the upper blackness. A tiny silhouetted form stood out against the holocaust and broken structures. It moved, and resembled a gnat. But to be visible at such a distance meant the thing had to be colossal. It was on three legs and moved along with purposeful strides. From being barely visible at first, the captain's eye became attuned to what was in the lenses of his binoculars. The nightmarish deformity became distinct, even though it danced and hovered within his breeze-whipped and shaking hands. Every breath he took caused a further struggle to keep the image in focus.

"Good God!" Chudleigh exclaimed. He had the nightmarish vision in view, too. "What the devil is that thing? Can you see it, Captain?"

"Yes, Number One. I have it in sight."

Quartermaster Middleton ran to the end of the superstructure and peered through his binoculars with his elbows resting on the guardrail. He scanned the illuminated horizon until his sweep came upon the tiny black outline of a dark ball with three hair-like legs. It moved with wicked grace across the tortured landscape, spewing flame at black ruins—buildings that had become dark columns, wretched, twisted and humbled, bowed in submission before the vile life form that paraded among them in its alien splendour.

He looked up to see Devour and Heinemann, who had followed them out of the bridge, standing beside him. All were fascinated and awed by the spectacle, which gradually receded as the ship continued its voyage.

"Over there," said Middleton, handing the binoculars to Devour. The Frenchman muttered his astonishment as he focused on the scene. He lingered for a few seconds, then gave the apparatus to Heinemann.

"Mein Gott," exclaimed the young German, his body stiffening at the sight within the lens. It was far off, but distinguishable. The aliens were real and happening in England. How long before they went onto the mainland, smashing, killing and burning a path across Europe and then into the other continents—spreading like a cancer across the planet, with nothing to stop them in all of man's arsenal of killing machinery?

"How will we ever stop these things?" Devour was of the same mind. The prospect before humanity was awesome, and there appeared to be no way of thwarting the imminent ruin that was all but upon them.

"I don't know, sir," muttered Middleton. "But prevail we must and will. These are early battles. They can't withstand shells when hit. We need to find ways of being able to hit the bastards. Ways of getting close enough to bang one home." He licked his lips and stared down at the panelled deck—his mind clicking over. "I know at least two of them have been downed. They got one a little while ago at Maidstone."

Heinemann's jaw locked firmly. "So we know they can die."

Middleton smiled back at the German officer. He liked the young man's mark. "Oh yes, sir, they die, and die they surely will. By hook or…"

"By crook." Heinemann locked his jaw fiercely.

"Well," added Devour mildly. "It's plain you are both of the same mind. I hope you're right, Quartermaster." He made his way to the semaphore, where the captain and commander were. Beside them was the signalman, pointing to the receding glimmer for the young boy seaman, who had borrowed his telescope. It seemed everyone was in on the act.

Behind Heinemann and Devour followed the quartermaster, now showing concern for the boy seaman.

"You all right, Perry lad?"

"Yes, Quartermaster," he replied, standing upright and giving the telescope back to the signalman.

"Good lad." He nodded his head, accepting that Perry didn't want to be relieved from the watch.

"New signals, sir," the signalman shouted, and instantly, all eyes were on the flickering light directly abeam as the ship cruised past the shore station.

23.35 Ashford destroyed by Martian onslaught. Many casualties. Refugees massing on both sides of the Thames. Chatem is full of newcomers. Situation critical. People demonstrative and fighting to get aboard vessels. Law and order breaking down.

"It's beginning," said Captain McIntosh. "Hysteria is gaining the upper hand, and reason is ebbing away."

A sudden salvo boomed across the night sky, and all turned aft where the cannonade had come from. Flickering lights and further cannon roar were seen and heard as they returned again to the rear of the superstructure.

"They're ours," said Chudleigh, holding his binoculars firmly as the fleet behind began to bombard the far off land where the burning was. "I can see *HMS Ceaser, Canopus* and *Magnificent*—all are firing at the inland burning. There are other ships, too, but I can't make them out."

"One of them is the *FS Courbet*," added Devour keenly.

Heinemann searched frenziedly with his own binoculars, homing in every time there was a flash—hoping and praying the *Konig Wilhelm* was among them. Suddenly, he made out her brief outline as the flash from her guns lit her up for a fraction of a second. It was all he needed to recognise his country's vessel and he called out triumphantly, "Our boys, too!" As all continued to peer through various magnifying apparatuses towards the far-off, apocalyptic glow, they saw the explosions. Earth was lifted amid the bursting flames of naval shells. Every shell seemed to fall just short of the vaguely discernible Martian construction. It was, however, awe inspiring and impressive – humans delivering hell to the Martians – a man-made ignition, as opposed to alien inferno, letting the extra-terrestrial know that Mother Earth had teeth.

"They'll get the range of that blooming thing soon. So help me God, they will," muttered Middleton with delight.

Perry gritted his teeth and smiled enthusiastically back at the proud quartermaster. His words were full of encouragement. For a moment the bombardment stopped, and Perry assumed the various ships were adjusting gun ranges and sights. A second salvo might do it. The chilling phenomenon might be destroyed before his very eyes. The fearfulness of the eerie sight was beginning to dull, and he was gripped by nervous excitement, the colossal sound of human shells, and good old human bile bubbling within. For a brief moment the Martian machine had lost its fear factor. It was now a distant thing, small through the telescope.

"Unfortunately, our muzzle-loading guns are not appropriate for this," remarked Chudleigh.

Captain McIntosh nodded agreement. "It's a shame. Still, perhaps we might see the others score a hit. Is that really what a Martian fighting machine looks like?"

"I think so, Captain," answered Chudleigh. "It seems to match the descriptions."

"At such a distance it does not look so formidable, yet there is clearly intense devastation about the thing. It's just standing amid that carnage, like a monument."

Suddenly, from the distant inferno where the Martian stood, a high pitched screech tore through the night air. At the same moment, a thin spear of light ripped across the land towards the sea and the trailing ships at the rear of Thunder Child. It was where the gun salvos had come from. The giant needle of light zipped over the convoy of battleships and sped off harmlessly into the night. The heat ray had missed.

"Good lord," muttered the Captain.

Then another screech tore out, and a further javelin of bright energy shot across the glowing land.

This time the bolt entered the covering darkness and bathed the trailing ships in a malicious glow before hitting the sea. The bolt pierced the water, trailing a hissing wake close to the shadowy outline of HMS Magnificent.

Then another bolt ripped across the water. This punctured the night with the same fury, but this time struck Magnificent amidships. The beam seemed to squirt across the land and sea.

The eruption was spectacular. The iron vessel was ripped apart in a blinding flame. Apocalypse was now at the midst of the convoy, a rude awakening to what the alien fighting machine could do.

Everyone on the Thunder Child's superstructure staggered as the ship shook under the unholy ball of fire from the stricken Magnificent at the rear. Thick wrought-iron and rivets had been torn to shreds, like paper. For a moment the night was gone, and all was bathed in a wicked orange radiance that lit the death of the stricken ship.

As though on cue, and with a renewed anger, the rest of the battleships, from various navies, once again opened up with a wild roar. More fire spat from their guns. Pure unadulterated and gorgeous hatred hurled hell and defiance at the invader, with its own cruel indifference.

Perry gathered his wits and stared through the bulwark-mounted telescope. Officers lifted their binoculars. Shells began to erupt about the Martian fighting machine. Earth, wind and fire seemed to engulf its blurred, alien structure, like a peculiar stage curtain that rose from the floor instead of dropping from above. The machine seemed to be at its point of destruction.

"They must have got the bastard," hissed Middleton.

"I think this time they have Quartermaster," said the Captain.

"I hope whatever is inside burns to hell," spat Chudleigh.

Behind them, the groan of HMS Magnificent could be heard, amid the clamour and calls of sailors in the water. Perry was shocked at the realisation that some men had actually survived the burning wreck. The intense glow was now fading. Gradually the fires were swallowed by an engulfing darkness and the blackness of the sea. The wreck was consumed as it receded into the dark bilge.

HMS Thunder Child cruised on into the sanctuary of the covering night. Her crew could do nothing as they left the fading shouts of wretched sailors, calling out in the darkness. There were many ships behind and hopefully better placed to pick up survivors.

McIntosh had to ignore the demise of Magnificent. He put a brave face on and smiled. "One for all, Lieutenant Devour…"

He lingered deliberately, waiting for the Frenchman to complete, but Heinemann was first.

"And all for one," he finished.

"Let's hope so."

Chudleigh smiled nervously and turned with the rest as they made their way back to the bridge, allowing the fleet behind to their bombardment. The captain doubted it would be of any use at such range and the likelihood of killing their own fleeing civilians was more real than hitting a Martian tripod. So they had seen the vague form of one at a distance. Still the Martians were an enigma—unreal—maybe a trick of the mind at such range because they had a vague idea of a shape they searched for, the eye and imagination could have forged the manifestation for them. No, the vessels behind, strafing the burning landscape, were closer and not everyone aboard all the ships would mistake such a phenomenon.

An urge to confront the aliens began to glow in McIntosh's chest—a yearning sparked from a small, yet buoyant radiance, one he felt growing steadily. The human race would prevail against the Martians—one way or another, they would come through this blight—and he knew that *HMS Thunder Child* would play a part in the matter.

He went back into the bridge with Chudleigh and the foreign liaison officers following like a bunch of love-struck puppies.

Middleton stayed put with Perry and the signal-man. "Grows more grotesque by the moment," he muttered to them

"The population must be in great panic at the moment. Everyone will want to get out of the country," added the signalman.

"I don't think we'll be able to cope," said Perry.

"Who's we, lad?" The quartermaster stared down at him.

"The navy, Quartermaster, every part of it. From Royal, merchant and rowing boats. I doubt with everything involved, we'd be able to evacuate everyone."

Middleton raised an eyebrow. "Evacuate ah mmm, lad." He was surprised by the boy seaman's use of words.

"Loves nice words, does our Boy Seaman Perry." The signalman had already found Perry's vocabulary impressive.

The quartermaster's moustache lifted on either side as his cheeks raised the clinging hair like bird wings, with his pointed nose for the body. The man was smiling, amused by the youngster before him. "Keep it up, young Perry. Such things lay well upon you. Don't forget that qualities like this get noticed, lad."

"Yes, Quartermaster." He was embarrassed by the compliment, but had the sense to know

Middleton was trying to build confidence in him. How different the man was from the first impression he got. He wondered if it had anything to do with the fall out with Jolly.

"Carry on then, lads," he added, then walked off to the conning tower and descended to the wheelhouse.

"You seem to have got onto his good side," said the signalman.

"You wouldn't have said that if you'd seen him when we left port." Perry smiled and then shook his head. "He seems to be keen on me learning the signals."

"Then do so. When Middleton takes you under his wing, it means he likes you and has confidence in your abilities. He surrounds himself with his own handpicked bunch and he looks after us, too. But we in turn make sure we're up to scratch and do everything efficiently. When he does his rounds, he's in heaven if we're performing to scratch—and if the quartermaster is in heaven, life's beautiful."

"And what if he's upset?" asked Perry.

"Do I really need to answer that one for you, Boy Seaman Perry? Surely you're not that green." He laughed at the mere thought of such a thing.

Perry grinned. "No, I think I know what you mean. Keep the quartermaster sweet and days will be sunny. Even when it's raining."

"Now you've got it."

They looked aft across the port quarterdeck where the red haze was barely visible along the rim of land. The distant fleet barrage had stopped and *Thunder Child* cruised on deep into the night, closing on the Isle of Sheppey, then westward around into the mouth of the Thames.

Mister Stanley at Southend Pier

He woke to a humming sound that he knew, instantly, had nothing whatever to do with the paddle steamer's engines. All about that early morning, mist hovered above the estuary, which he knew was flat and calm—despite the fact he couldn't see the water. *The Southend Belle* appeared to be drifting through the thick morning mist towards the distant buzz.

"What is it?" asked Daisy Wade who, through his fidgeting, had woken. All three had been huddled together beneath a blanket with little Jojo in the middle, still sleeping soundly.

"I've no idea," replied Mister Stanley. "But it is most unusual indeed."

She looked down at the wooden deck as though trying to fathom whether it was coming from the vessel. "It's not the boat, Albert."

He looked into the mist and said. "It sounds like the House of Commons when it is silent, or Saint Paul's Cathedral."

"Yes, a big enclosed space with the distant whispering of people..." She stopped abruptly.

Then as one, they both said, "It's people!" They looked into the mist.

"Lots of people—loads in the distance," added Mister Stanley.

Suddenly, there was the sound of distant bells and the paddle steamer's foghorn blew, waking Jojo with a fright. She screamed out in her sleep and was brought into the wicked world where she had been robbed of her parents just one day previous.

"It's all right, little petal," replied Daisy as she picked the little girl up and cuddled her tightly. Jojo buried her head into the soft comforting mound and sobbed while her trembling body gradually subsided. "There, there, petal, it will be all right."

Mister Stanley put a gentle hand on the infant's shoulder and rubbed soothingly. He didn't have much experience with children, but was distressed by the little girl's trauma. How he wished he could do more for both her, and Daisy Wade. Why was it that in a world of nightmares he'd discovered strong affection and a fierce competitive drive to protect? Part of him dared not wish for normality, where he would never have had such an encounter; if in a world of nightmare he had met his desired destiny, then from that world he would safely bring them. His jaw was resolute as he vowed to himself: "Nothing will harm them,"

But he kept promise inside his head, where only God could hear.

"Oh my Lord!" Daisy muttered.

Mister Stanley turned and followed her line of vision. The mist was beginning to clear and before them an iron-stilted structure came out of the still glass-faced sea—its length disappearing into the thickness of the mist. Upon it was a mass of people, who were climbing down ladders and descending ramps onto sea vessels of all kinds. There was pushing and shoving as children were hauled over the heads of the mass and onto the boats—some crying out for parents left upon the framework.

"We are at the end of Southend Pier," said Mister Stanley.

"My word, the place must be full with thousands of people." Daisy cuddled little Jojo to her in case the spectacle before them caused the infant further trauma. "I bet the entire pier is packed all the way back to the shore."

Mister Stanley turned to her. "It's over a mile long." He couldn't imagine such a horde of people, but as the morning mist began to clear and more of the pier's length became visible, the evidence was all too obvious. "Good Lord! There must be many thousands of people on the pier alone."

"There are soldiers and sailors keeping them in check," she added, watching the armed men policing the crowd as best they could.

"And the small boats are ferrying people out to the ships and steamers."

"Yes, look at them all. The poor, wretched souls."

One of the boats came towards *The Southend Belle*. It was full of women and children all from different social standings—the affluent among the poor—no first or second class citizens. Just people trying to evade and survive the dread of the Martian tripods.

"Its complete bedlam, Daisy. The whole world has gone stark raving mad."

"What is to become of us, Albert?" She reached for his hand, which he willingly gave her.

Squeezing her hand, he whispered soothingly. "One way or another, Daisy, you, Jojo and I are going to come through this." His jaw was locked determinedly and she squeezed his hand back, drawing comfort from his bold resolve.

"I've come to have great faith in you, Albert."

He smiled. "Thank you. I won't let you down."

They could hear the people being brought aboard—the chatter coming from below deck and before long, the first groups came up onto the open deck and found places for themselves. As time went on, the steamer became full and the hum and chatter was all around.

Mister Stanley and Daisy Wade sat holding hands and watching the events unfold, while little Jojo once again, lay sleeping—her head to the side against Daisy's ample breasts. The infant's long hair covered her small, innocent face, hiding from the mad world.

"The mist has cleared," muttered Daisy.

Mister Stanley looked about startled. "My word, so it has." He had been wrapped up in watching the women and children come aboard. "Good God, I've never seen so many people in my life."

He stood in amazement as he scanned the length of the pier. It was crammed for over a mile with dense humanity, jostling and pushing to be near the small vessels moored at the bottom of the ugly criss-cross configuration of metal girders that came up from the still sea. He looked along the seafront, too, and was further bewildered by the many thousands upon the beach and promenade.

"It's an absolute sea of humanity," he muttered. "Where on earth do all these people think they can go?"

"What makes any of us think the Martian tripod machines won't be where we choose to run? They fall from the sky. They must surely be falling abroad, too." Daisy was becoming more anxious.

They were there for many hours, and none could make out why the larger boats couldn't go and moor next to the pier. Mister Stanley asked a passing crewman for an explanation.

"Well, sir," began the man. "Look at the desperate plight of everyone on the pier. It's women and children first you see, and a big boat alongside will cause a mad rush. It might seem a fruitless waste of time, but the navy and army boys can keep people at bay, plus make sure women and children get ferried across first. The situation is very serious, sir, and someone is likely to get shot."

"Oh," replied Mister Stanley bemused. He sat back and watched the sailor leave. "Well, Daisy, I think we might be here for some time yet."

As the morning wore on, the mist began to clear, *The Southend Belle* started her engines and began to paddle away from the pier, which was still crammed with masses of people. Another paddle steamer was to port and also began to move away with its decks laden with people, crushed to the bulwarks.

"Look, Jojo, another steamer, just like ours," said Daisy, trying to keep the little girl's mind occupied.

"It is very much like ours, isn't it, Jojo?" added Mister Stanley, trying to let the infant know she had their attention.

Jojo murmured some sort of agreement and pointed towards the packed paddle steamer.

"It is called *The Walton Belle*," said Daisy. "Can you say that, Jojo?"

Jojo looked up and replied "Bell-bell."

"Very good," beamed Daisy.

It was then that a change came over all—a silence that cut through the air leaving a momentary stillness—a small hiccup in time, and followed by a new air of panic that swept across the estuary.

"Something's wrong," said Daisy, as the panic became evident among all the refugees aboard the boat.

Mister Stanley stood up amid the commotion. "What on earth could it be?"

He looked to the shore where the tall white Pier Hotel sat by the hill that came down along the coastline and the distant scream came above the rooftops.

"Aloo, aloo."

He turned and looked to Daisy, who was shaking while Jojo began to cry and cuddle into her. Kneeling before them, he wrapped his arms around both and hugged them tightly.

CHAPTER 10

PANIC IN THE THAMES ESTUARY

"Up, up!"
The clanging bell ripped through many a man's sleep and the siren was wailing.

"All hands on deck. All hands on deck."

Sailors cursed and pushed at one another, but somehow managed to fall out in order, coming out on the open deck and manning their stations. To port was the Isle of Sheppey with the Kent coast westwards, while to starboard the town of Southend with its long pier stretching out into the estuary. It was a hive of activity, and boats of all sizes were along the sides of the structure. Many large vessels were beached on the mud flats with decks crammed full of people eagerly waiting for the tide to lift them. Queues stretched from the crowded shore out onto the banks, and officials were directing groups to various vessels. Small inlets cut into the banks—wrays, as the locals called them. Here, the little fishing smacks traversed, with people jammed on their decks.

"Christ! Now what do they want?" cursed Jolly as he came out upon the open deck.

Pickles was by his side in an instant:

"They've had signals from the shore station. There's a temporary one on the hill by Hadleigh Castle."

He pointed to the hill, where woodland and fields surrounded the derelict Norman tower and its surrounding rubble. It overlooked the estuary where the river Thames flowed into the North Sea. Close by was a Royal Navy signal unit with its sema-phore active.

Pickles gasped. "They reckon one of the blight-ers is on its way."

"What, a Martian?" Jolly's tone was half afraid, but also bore a degree of ridicule.

"Well, blooming hell, if I never..." said Boatswain Pickles. "I've never seen so many people in all my life."

Jolly nodded, a plaster across the bridge of his nose—two black eyes and a swollen lip. "I can't believe it. The bloody arcades are booming with business, look!"

Pickles scrutinised the shore, where hordes of people moved along the seafront and to his utter surprise, he saw the amusement arcades were full. "Well I never..." he muttered in disbelief. "People are the absolute limit. Who would have thought that anyone could think of such things during times like this?"

"Beat's me, Bosun. People do behave strangely during unpredictable circumstances, but that's taken me by surprise."

They stood at the bulwarks of the main deck while the rest of the crew were running about to their stations.

Pickles raised an eyebrow and turned to Jolly—a deep frown etched across his forehead. "Even you, aye, Jolly? Well, wonders will never cease. You're with me, aren't you?"

"Yes, sir, the quartermaster told me to report to you."

"Good, Jolly, you're going to the engine room to learn a little about main engine throttles and the telegraph order receiving, so listen good because it will be to your advantage if you show aptitude, do you understand me, lad?

"Yes, Bosun," he replied, wondering what he had done to earn such a change of fortune. "Is this what the quartermaster had in mind for me when he told me to report to you, Bosun?"

"He did." The reply was abrupt as he sauntered off, with Jolly following behind like a humble and grateful servant. Unbeknown to himself, he had scored some merit with Middleton when he insisted he had fallen down the ladder way to receive his face injury. The old quartermaster knew what had happened, but was happy to indulge this petty type of honour among the crewmen.

"Well now, I'm rather pleased about that, Bosun."

"And so you should be, you lily-livered Nancy. You don't get plum numbers like this crop up all the time, so make sure you're worthy of it."

Jolly ambled behind the boatswain, unable to believe his good fortune. "Oh I will at that, Bosun, I can assure you."

They stopped and looked towards the shore as a ripple of hysteria ran along the seafront—the crowd as a single entity had become alarmed and began to panic. The noise rose as the undulating mass surged over the sea wall and onto the beach like a swarm of locusts. Spilling out like liquid, the expanse of humanity spread onto the mud flats.

Beyond the town's rooftops there was a bobbing movement; the top of something white sparkled, then sank, only to rise again with each unseen stride. The colossal crash of each step shook through the streets to the sea as the thing drew closer.

"Aloo…" The screech ripped across the estuary.

"Good God, look where the pier begins," Boatswain Pickles pointed. "The road that goes up the hill into the town centre."

The monolithic alien machine came into view at the top of Pier Hill beside the white grandeur of the Palace Hotel. Its huge dirty white trunk was framed by the clear blue expanse of the summer sky. Above, seagulls circled as though expectant of something—as though they followed in a ship's wake. For a moment, it swayed on its colossal legs, surveying the pandemonium before it.

"Aloo... Aloo!" The ghastly abomination resonated with excitement and a sinister blood lust.

Terrified screaming tore across the sea, as all fled before the gigantic predator. Some, by the tripod's feet, pathetically pressed themselves to walls in a feeble attempt to become one with the brickwork. Fortunately, the hideous titan was not interested in them.

The armoured trunk turned from east to west, pondering its next course of action. A green compound orb looked as though it might burst from the trunk's white alloy. Whether or not it was organic was difficult to judge at such a distance. Three limbs protruded from the body, ascending to mechanical joints, like human elbows, from where they lowered, forming long spiderlike legs that gave the Martian fighting machines their enormous height. It was impossible to tell what that creature looked like inside the machine from this distance.

The klaxon whirred as *Thunder Child*'s crew began running to action stations. The fore and aft turrets turned to starboard, towards the alien monstrosity.

Suddenly, to everyone's surprise, the tripod turned west and began to walk along the top of the steep grass cliffs. Its trunk was visible above the trees and in front of the rows of tall guesthouses. It went towards Westcliff and Chalkwell, outer districts of Southend.

"Bloody hell! Where's it going?" Jolly was shaken by the sight of the thing.

"It's not interested in anything here." Pickles looked westwards along the estuary and saw a multitude of fishing smacks winding along the inlets in the mud banks towards the open river. "Look down there. The cockle-fishing town, Leigh-on-Sea. It's interested in the small craft."

"What about us? There are bigger vessels here." Jolly was puzzled by the tripod's action, though his fast-beating heart was calming down a little and his fear starting to subside.

"Come on, lad, we've got to get down into the engine room..." Pickles tried to snap into the task of running the ship, but was cut short as a *whooshing* sound caused him to stop in his tracks. The discord fanned out across the estuary as the heat-ray zipped from the top of the tripod's trunk—a line of concentrated energy flashed, and a boom fanned out across the estuary.

The leading Peter boat went up in a ball of flames. It seemed at first an insignificant and unimpressive sight. Jolly noticed crew members looking to one another, searching for some sort of reaction before turning back to the smoke that was rising from the wreckage. Jolly sensed the entire crew thinking "Is that it?" There followed a brief, eerie silence as hundreds of thousands hushed, watching the distant spectacle in disbelief.

A second screech tore through the silence and across the estuary as a flash of energy shot from the tripod again. Another explosion followed, and a second vessel disappeared in an orange ball of flame. Then a third, and fourth—more in rapid succession—as waves of screams and panic spread across the estuary and the multitude cried out in dismay.

Suddenly, the horrific spectacle was smashing down the failed significance of the first Peter boat casualty. Fishing vessels, crowded with helpless refugees, were erupting and being engulfed in fiery orange bubbles that devoured everything and everyone in violent wholesale slaughter. No quarter was given to anyone that came under the scrutiny of the Martian tripod—an apocalyptic arbiter delivering death to all who attempted to flee.

Thunder Child's powerless crew could only watch in total disbelief—aghast at the startling display of mayhem and murder unfolding before them.

Soon, the mud flats were an inferno and the inlet became a line of fire. All the fishing boats were blazing away. Human screams swept the coastline.

Some people at the end of the inlet managed to jump from their vessels onto the mud banks and began desperately to run out across the flats. Their legs sank deeper with each step. The spectacle unfolded of fleeing people being systematically slaughtered trying to run across the entrapping silt. Their screams dispersed throughout as the heat-ray harvested the human wheat, shaking the multitude who watched on helplessly. Perhaps some survived, but most eyes were spellbound by the hideous spectacle of the vanquished. It had happened so fast and suddenly.

Leigh-on-Sea's old wharf and cockle-fishing smacks were part of a holocaust, spewing smoke that spread its defilement into the blue apocalyptic sky. The horror brought instant and corrupt change to the summer day.

Along the Southend seafront, people began to stampede back into the town centre. Everyone wanted to be away from the tripod, which clearly had an aversion to people leaving the land.

Thunder Child's horn blew and at once, her engines came on, the propellers kicked into motion as she swung about and made her way east, out of the estuary towards the open sea, leaving the carnage and terror behind them.

Boatswain Pickles looked about in disbelief. "Good God, we're running. Leaving those poor devils helpless."

"I don't think there's anything we can do, Bosun. Look at those fishing boats."

A wall of flame stood behind the tripod as it turned and came back, but this time, striding out onto the mud flaps coming towards the pier.

"Christ!" cursed Jolly. "I don't believe this. The thing's going for the pier."

"Good God! Look at all the people on there," muttered Pickles.

More screams fanned out from the multitude that packed the long structure. Ships hastily began to pull away as gangplanks dropped into the sea. Some of the quick thinking people stranded on the pier, jumped into the water, supposing their chances would be better. Others, wretched and blind with fear, panicked. They surged like bugs upon a rose stem, knowing their fate if caught. Families gathered and clutched one another, terrified of being separated in the mass panic.

The heat-ray screeched and a thin line of flame shot out and hit a paddle steamer attempting to disembark. Again, the flames ballooned from the deck, engulfing the funnel, while the mast and rigging slowly toppled into the sea. Desperate passengers clambered over the side—some now human torches.

More screeching bursts of energy sang out, high-pitched grating, as *Thunder Child* cruised away towards the open sea.

The entire one-and-a-third mile length of the pier structure was a scene of complete chaos—thousands were gripped in blind panic. Hundreds began plunging into the sea as one by one, the moored boats and paddle steamers began to disembark.

The alien structure seemed to deploy a body language that portrayed astonishment. It reared slightly as its legs stiffened. Its funnelled weapon above the body trunk pointed down at the scattering vessels.

"Aloo ugh." The alien cry tore defiantly across the estuary. A bolt of energy flashed like a straight lightning bolt and another paddle steamer erupted in a ball of flame. Wood splinters and rigging lifted into the sky, then veered out into a descending trajectory that brought them crashing into the sea at sporadic and scattered intervals. Parts of the pier's framework began to explode as the tripod came above it and spewed its pulsating ray into the construction. The creature within the machine must have been manic in its slaughter. Every now and then, it would let its attention stray back to the flee-ing vessels and fire a few energy bolts at them. Each shot culminating in the destruction of a boat or a paddle steamer, before going back to the human panic upon the burning pier.

"Jesus," screamed Jolly. "Can't we shoot at the thing? Why ain't the guns firing?"

"No good from here, boy," Pickles was coming to grips with himself. "We're more likely to kill our own and then we'll be destroyed. What's happening out there will go on with or without our help."

For a moment, Jolly felt relieved as the aft turret began to rotate—its guns pointing towards the pier. "At blooming last."

"They're just covering our retreat, lad. Nothing else, and they won't fire unless that thing comes after us. The pier and its docked boats are doomed. All we can do is hope some of those poor devils get away." He looked about him. "We're the only Royal Naval vessel here. Everything else is out at sea."

Looking over the bow, lines of steam could be seen coming from the fleet that was just over the horizon.

"Why don't they come in land and have a go?" Jolly was getting more frustrated as he ran back along the main deck to the aft turret and looked back over the stern, where the flaming chaos upon the pier continued.

"There's nothing we can do, lad. Nothing at all."

They watched on as the pier erupted into flames, and the screaming faded as the distance between them grew. *Thunder Child* had left the civilians to the mercy of the Martian tripod, and no one would be able to make it out.

Beyond the flames, Pickles made out the hill where Hadleigh Castle's ruins overlooked the sea approach. The semaphore was still signalling to them beyond and above the fires.

Thunder Child must not engage. Proceed to River Blackwater by Clacton and observe ships there. Do not engage. Repeat. Do not engage.

"We've been ordered to leave," muttered Pickles as he deciphered the signals coming from the station by Hadleigh Castle.

"What!" Jolly couldn't believe what he heard. He looked to the semaphore position and also noticed the tripod's trunk turning from the flaming pier before it looked back to the devastation of Leigh. Its cylinder lifted up on a wire that had some form of spine. Suddenly, there was the by now familiar *whoosh*, coupled with a screech as a thin strand of energy leapt the two, maybe three mile distance engulfing the signal station in a ball of flame and slinging chunks of the old Norman ruin into the sky.

Every man aboard jumped. If the Martian could hit that target, then *Thunder Child* was also within range. But, no—the tripod walked to the shore and up Pier Hill and disappeared beyond the roof tops as it went back into the town centre, where more screaming and the whoosh of its ray was heard until the vessel was out into the open sea.

Behind, two of the paddle steamers, *The Southend Belle* and *The Walton Belle*, followed. Their paddle wheels whipped into the sea furiously while carrying wretched hoards of humanity pressed tightly against the guardrails. Each funnel spewed black smoke, while below the furnaces devoured heaps of coal in the eagerness to put distance between themselves and the mainland.

"Come on, girls. You can do it," muttered Pickles.

Shouts of encouragement rose from the crew, as they all became inflamed with a passion to see the two vessels make it into the open sea.

"Go on there, girls," they screamed encouragingly at the plucky little paddle steamers—sightseeing vessels for the day-trippers that visited the seaside resort.

Suddenly, there came a malicious cry from the retreating town of Southend-on-Sea.

"Aloo ugh."

The tripod had returned and was standing on the top of Pier Hill. The flaming town about it was like a decorative mantel to the demon. It was like a spoilt child that looked on as though upset by the sight of the paddle steamers that had eluded it. Again, the wires above its trunk raised and the cylinders attached pointed out at sea towards the fleeing vessels.

A roaring hum came from *Thunder Child* as the crew looked up at the ship's superstructure.

"What's that?" Jolly sounded fearful.

"We're making smoke," replied Pickles as a huge black cloud began to trail back over their wake towards the two steamers. "If they can reach the cloud, then the poor blighters might stand a chance."

A ripping screech cut through the air like lightening. There followed a blinding line of straight, luminous energy that *whooshed* across the estuary. The sea was torn up behind the stern of *The Walton Belle*, bisecting her wake, leaving a line of hot, boiling sea that hissed in protest until the angry froth was overrun by the clamour of the surrounding cold water.

The refugees aboard began to panic and those at the stern began to push towards the bow, causing a crush. There were screams of protest from all, including the crew of *Thunder Child*, in an earnest effort to bring order to them.

Suddenly, a second screech tore through the air. The *whoosh* barely registered as the ray smashed amidships of the paddle steamer. A crushed multitude of protesting humanity was there one moment, then vanished in a blinding explosion—swallowed in the fireball that inflated like an orange ball up and out across the sea, scattering debris before it.

The deafening roar and force lifted Jolly and Pickles, smashing them against the superstructure's wall.

"Good God," screamed Pickles, clutching his bruised ribs. He looked back as the flames climbed higher into the blue sky, while all about, the sea was splashing as cascading debris was scattered in all directions, some of it human.

The Southend Belle desperately began to zigzag as it entered *Thunder Child*'s covering black smoke to become engulfed. One energy bolt shot into the dark cloud in pursuit, but only the sound of the bubbling sea could be heard.

Jolly shook his head, unable to believe what he had seen. The flaming edifice of *The Walton Belle* was still roaring as it suddenly capsized, to be dragged down by the hungry sea—Mother Earth claiming her own.

Thunder Child swerved slightly to starboard and caused the smoke to fall across its wake like a veil and continued to cruise out into the open sea. *The Southend Belle* suddenly emerged from the covering soot, and just like the ironclad, on the blind side of the Martian.

"She's done it," said Pickles.

Jolly looked up, traumatised with tears in his bruised eyes. He shook his head in disbelief.

"Come on, lad." Pickles helped him up. "Let's get down into the engine room."

He stood and followed the boatswain without a word of protest. Behind and beyond the smoke cloud, amid the clamorous roar of burning buildings and screaming people, Southend-on-Sea burned. There were more distant screeches signalling the firing of the heat-ray followed by the *whoosh* and explosion of what had been hit. The seaside town was left to its fate.

Mister Stanley's Soothing Words

"It's alright now, we've done it," sobbed Mister Stanley as he cuddled Daisy and Jojo into him. He had seen *The Walton Belle* blow up just as they had entered the cover of *Thunder Child*'s smoke. It had almost broken him and he thanked God that Jojo's head had been buried into his body and she hadn't seen it.

"Oh my word, Albert." Daisy held her hand to her mouth in utter dismay. "I can't believe this is happening. What horrid things—what can we do to stop them?"

All around them, other refugees were blaspheming in anger and terror.

"We've got to do something," cursed an angry Irish woman. "We'll find a way. We have to and when we do, we'll show them..."

"Hear, hear," shouted another women, in wealthy dress.

As one, many of the refugees began ranting and cursing at the black smoke barrier, beyond which the alien monstrosity lurked. They began chanting and cursing the enigma of the Martian tripods. Then they began to sing "Onwards Christian Soldiers". The paddle steamer made its way out of the estuary into the open sea, where the huge dreadnought battleships were with others from foreign navies.

Mister Stanley looked into Daisy's soft brown eyes and the wrinkled curls that hung around her face. He was pleased she was still with him, and grateful little Jojo was cuddled into him for comfort. He was warmed by their need for him and they, in turn, were essential to him.

Daisy smiled and put her hand to his face. "We must not be apart, Albert," she whispered, with tears swelling in her eyes.

He shook his head. "Perish the thought, Daisy. I can't contemplate such a thing."

"We will stay together? All three of us." She looked down at little Jojo. The infant was confused by the way her small world had changed, but was quickly adapting to Mister Stanley and Daisy as her guardians.

"She is very young," said Mister Stanley. "She will get used to us."

Daisy looked to the fore of the steamer. "We seem to be heading for one of the bigger ships out there." She looked to Mister Stanley solemnly.

"What's wrong, Daisy?" He read her look.

"I don't want us to go to a foreign country where the same things are just as likely to be, Albert."

"I agree. If they aren't there yet, they soon will be. We can't keep running forever. There has to be some way around this."

"Can't we get off when this boat returns to the land? It might go back to Kent and then we can return to my cottage."

Mister Stanley sighed. It was a tempting thing and he was sure that wherever they went there would be Martian tripods. "Why should Belgium or France be tripod free? We're being very arrogant in assuming Britain is the only place of interest to creatures from out of space. Maybe as an island, we're a first stop—a place easy enough to secure— before they move on."

"Do you think we are the first, or do you believe they're already landing abroad?" She looked across the sea to *Thunder Child* and was comforted by the small ironclad's presence.

"Well, I do question why we have foreign battle-ships out there with our own. If the Martians were in other countries, then surely these nations' ships would be guarding their own coastlines." He was perplexed, and shook his head as he tried to fathom it all out.

"I'm quite happy to stay on the paddle steamer," added Daisy. "I'm not sure if I want to go abroad."

"We'll stay then. I'm not going to ask anyone, just in case they order us to leave. We'll stow away some-where, or at least become obscure until the boat returns back to the land. It will not be Southend, of that I'm sure."

"I think much of it might be destroyed by now." She looked back at the receding estuary towards the distant flames and smoke rising from Southend-on-Sea. Concern was etched into her face, and she was desperate. "Now more than anything, I know I do not want to go abroad. This is the furthest away from my country's coastline I have been and I don't want to go any further. What trials and tribulations lie ahead, I cannot say, but I would sooner face them in Britain." She took little Jojo from Mister Stanley with a gentle smile and hugged her tightly.

He moved forward boldly and put his arms around both of them. He felt wonderful—strong and unafraid—for Daisy Wade had brought some-thing out in him that he would never have realised he possessed. The whole sordid and terrible affair had brought him good fortune. He had done things with an initiative he never would have thought he had and, in the process, he had met the wonderful widow who stood before him. It is often said that during traumatic times obscure people can do great things, and at this particular moment, Mister Stanley was feeling very proud indeed.

"We will stay here and we will survive this. It's not over yet, Daisy, and those horrid things will get their comeuppance. One way or another, they will. You mark my words." He leaned over and kissed her forehead, then relaxed from his momentary little impulse.

Daisy smiled back at him and said, "We will survive, Albert, because God wouldn't let me find someone as wonderful as you and take him away. We're too old to have children of our own, but we would make wonderful parents. Do you not think so?"

His heart leapt with joy—how wonderful she was. "Indeed I do, Daisy. Let us make a vow that we will come through this and always be together and raise little Jojo as our daughter. Daisy, will you marry me?" He stopped and looked away—suddenly embarrassed at his overexcitement. What if she refused him?

"Yes, Albert, I will. I don't ever want to be without you." Her voice engulfed him in rapture—a soft aura smothered him with a wonderful sense of belonging.

When he looked back at her, there were happy tears in each other's eyes. She leaned forward and gently kissed him. As she stood back smiling, she said, "Despite everything, I wouldn't change things for the world—not for an entire war of the world, Albert."

"Never in a million years," agreed Mister Stanley.

CHAPTER 11

FOLLOWING THE SOUTHEND BELLE

*T*hunder Child stayed at the side of the sole surviving paddle steamer as it went out into the
sea, where an armada of ships cruised north. Every
crewman was trying to calm himself after the
traumatic events that had occurred. Many of *The
Southend Belle*'s refugees were still lamenting the loss
of *The Walton Belle*.

The Royal Navy, with all its might, wouldn't venture into the estuary. *Thunder Child* had been the
only military vessel to do so.

"I can't make it out," said Brandt, the port signalman, to Perry. "The amount of clout that lot
have got and they send us in. *Thunder Child* is an
outdated, coastal defence ship with muzzle-loading
guns. Why us?"

"I expect they must have a reason, and seeing what that blooming thing did to all the fishing boats and steamers, well…" Perry lingered and shook his head.

"Well what?" asked Brandt.

Perry looked up at him. "I reckon it would have made just as quick work of anything we could put up against it."

Brandt sighed. "Maybe you're right. Christ!" he cursed through clenched teeth. "If only we could get one of the things in our sights. BOOM!" The clap of his hands died in the wind.

"Wow," exclaimed Perry. "Look at that thing."

An armoured French cruiser broke off from the convoy and approached with a British battleship escorting behind.

"The Frog ship's called *FS Dupuy de Lome* and ours is *The Royal Sovereign*," said Brandt.

Even without the familiar tricolour, Perry would have guessed the ship to be French because of her shape, which was like that of the *FS Courbet* where Lieutenant Devour had come from.

Again Brandt spoke. "A lot of French ships look like that, with the old cutaway bow and stern. I've seen other nations with similar designs, but they always turn out to be ships made in France."

"I think she's making for *The Southend Belle*," said Perry.

"And *Royal Sovereign* wants us. She's coming this way."

"She's signalling," added Perry.

"That's for the starboard semaphore," scolded Brandt flippantly. "We deal with portside only."

The French cruiser and *The Southend Belle* passed on starboard sides, but then the *FS Dupuy de Lome* turned majestically, cutting a sharp path astern to come abeam between *Thunder Child*'s starboard side and the paddle steamer's port. She completely obscured the little vessel from view, but the crew of *Thunder Child* knew the refugees were being taken aboard.

"You know that cruiser was built as a commerce raider because France thought she might soon be at war with Britain. Now look, she's aiding us." Brandt shook his head. "Bet they never thought they'd be helping us fight Martians."

Both turned and watched as Captain McIntosh emerged from the bridge. Behind him, Chudleigh and Devour followed. They went to the starboard semaphore.

"The captain is looking fatigued," said Perry.

"In respect of the recent events, I think he might be entitled."

To Perry's surprise, the starboard semaphore was taking signals from *The Royal Sovereign* and the *Dupuy de Lome*. His interest grew when he noticed the French liaison officer shake his head in disbelief.

"There seems to be a bit of a commotion over there." Brandt studied curiously.

Captain McIntosh and Lieutenant Devour began talking excitedly, turning to Chudliegh, who was shaking his head with the same look of bewilderment. More instructions were given to the starboard signalman, who began working the semaphore.

"I think they're trying to get confirmation of something," said Brandt. "I think the captain wants to make sure of something. I wonder what it could be?"

"Christ, I'd love to know what it is," agreed Perry.

Once the captain and his officers were satisfied with the ratification from both ships, they went back into the bridge.

"What was that all about?" Brandt called across.

The starboard semaphore crew shrugged unsure, then the messenger replied. "Something about going to the Blackwater with the paddle steamer."

"And picking up some important people carrying something," added the starboard signalman.

The messenger looked at the bridge door to make sure no one was coming out and then, like a naughty schoolboy, walked halfway across and whispered something Perry and Brandt couldn't fathom.

"I can't hear you," replied Brandt.

The starboard messenger's face contorted in frustrated annoyance. He took another look at the bridge hatch, which was still shut. Finally, he took a few more steps towards them and whispered loud enough for them to hear above the sea.

"Among the people is a French professor, who has been at Colchester University. He's with some pupils and they have been studying germs."

"What sort of germs?" asked Brandt bemused. Perry nodded his support. It was all very strange.

"I heard flu, chicken pox and measles," replied the messenger and then he quickly returned to his post by the starboard semaphore.

"What the blooming hell 'as that got to do with all this?" Brandt shook his head in disbelief.

Again, Perry nodded his agreement. "What are we going to do? Blooming sneeze on them?"

For about half-an-hour, they called across to one another and speculated about things and invented all sorts of probabilities, but at the end none of them could fathom out the importance of this French professor.

The *Dupuy de Lome* brought them out of their theorising as her propellers began to churn up the sea at her stern. She had taken all refugees aboard and was heading back to the convoy of shipping. At her side, *The Royal Sovereign* cruised—both vessels leaving a foamed wake.

The Southend Belle, now empty of passengers, looked light and fragile as she bobbed up and down in the waves. Some of her crew moved about on deck and were calling across to sailors on *Thunder Child*'s quarterdeck. They appeared to be laughing at what was going on. They evidently knew they would be going back to the Essex coast and along the Blackwater.

Brandt shook his head in disbelief. "They seem in fine spirits after what they've just been through."

"The laughter is nervous. They're putting on brave faces."

Perry strained his ears in the hope of getting some more information, but could make out none of the chatter.

"Maldon," said Brandt, feeling a little aggrieved that some young wet neck would correct him. "I heard someone say 'near Maldon'."

"Is that where we're supposed to pick up the French professor and his little bag of germs?"

Brandt couldn't answer, as everyone had to look sharp about their business. Quartermaster Middleton had stepped out of the bridge. There appeared a smirk upon his face and he knew his men had been gossiping.

"Well now. Are we all looking sharp and ready for anything that might come along?" he boomed.

Oh dear, thought Perry. The quartermaster was in that old familiar joking mood and Perry didn't quite know how to handle the man when he was like this. There always seemed to be deviousness under the surface when the words 'Well now' were put at the front of Middleton's sentences.

"What's been going on then, young Perry?"

The quartermaster wanted an answer and Perry wasn't going to mess the man about.

"We were wondering if we are to go back in shore, Quartermaster, along the Blackwater."

To everyone's relief, Middleton smiled and calmness swept over his face. He looked to the starboard semaphore, knowing the men there must have been chatting about the signals they had received for the captain. A smile creased his face and he nodded his head as he looked back to Perry and Brandt.

"We are at that, boy. I want all you lads to keep mum about it where the rest of the crew are concerned. Understood?"

"Yes, Quartermaster," they bellowed.

"Good lads. That one is a specific from the captain, so don't let me down now, will you, boys?"

"No, Quartermaster." And they meant it.

Middleton went to the conning tower and slid down the ladder way to the steering position. He was gone as quick as he appeared.

"Well, Perry," whispered Brandt. "You handled things properly and didn't try to con your way out. He likes that and now I know he wants you among us. He treats us good, but we look after him, too. Everything we do up here is done to the best of our ability. Don't mess up with him 'cause, believe me, you got your bleeding foot in the door, mate."

Perry smiled, pleased he was establishing a niche for himself. His confidence was growing all the time and he was warming to the idea of being reliable.

"Will I learn the semaphore?" he asked hopefully.

"Of course." Brandt smiled briefly, but his face stiffened as he looked back at the Essex coast. "I don't much fancy going back. Not after what happened at Southend."

"Maybe they haven't got to the Blackwater yet?" Perry suggested.

"Judging by what we've all seen of Martians, I think it would be safe to assume they are capable of getting there quicker than we can."

Perry went quiet. He had to agree that Brandt was right. For a moment, a strange calm settled and only the tranquil sea could be heard lapping against *Thunder Child*'s hull. The rest of the world had retreated so that he might ponder what lay before them—a placid lull, before an oncoming upheaval that loomed just beyond the horizon.

Mister Stanley Stays Aboard The Southend Belle

"Well, that went easier than I had anticipated," said Mister Stanley as they came back up onto the open deck again. They had picked an obscure place below and just sat there while everyone else boarded the French battleship for evacuation.

"I'm surprised no one asked us what we were doing," agreed Daisy.

"I don't suppose it occurred to them that people might want to go back." He looked gratefully to the Essex coastline, which was moving by the portside as the paddle steamer made its way northwards.

"Well, it's too late for them to do anything about it now." Daisy was watching the *FS Dupuy de Lome* shrinking into the midst of the other shipping as the distance between them increased.

"We've passed the Thames estuary, and we're now heading up coast. I wonder where we'll be going now?"

Suddenly, there came a shout from a crewman who had spotted them from his work point at the bow. He was looking up at them as they moved to the front rail of the upper deck. "Oy! What are you people still doing on board?"

Mister Stanley played the fool and pretended it was a strange question to be asking. "I beg your pardon, young man."

"What are you doing aboard?" he repeated the question.

"Do not address me as 'Oy', young man, and we are aboard because we were kindly picked up by the captain at Herne Bay."

The young man was suddenly mindful of his manners and on the defensive—suddenly feeling out of his depth and not in control, he replied:

"Well, sir, everyone was meant to go aboard the *FS Dupuy de Lome.*"

"My good man, I am from the War Office and have been attached to the Royal Navy involving land signal stations since this crisis began. I am not a refugee and did not come aboard as a refugee. Like young Seaman Lawrence, who was a part of my shore party, I am meant to be here and this lady and child are in my care."

"Oh," replied the crewman. "Begging your pardon and all, sir, I didn't realise."

"Not realising is fine, young man, but adopt a more kindly approach than 'Oy'. It tends to get one's back up."

"Beg your pardon, sir, and begging your pardon, lady."

The young hand went back about his business without even bothering to report it to the captain. The Royal Navy man had come aboard with the War Office man and the lady with the child at Herne Bay and he was different from the rest of the refugees that had boarded at the pier. He was concerned that his bad-mannered approach might be reported.

"Well, you can fool some people all the time and all people some of the time," added Daisy with a hint of admiration. "How long do you think it will last until the next one comes along?"

"Well it doesn't really matter anymore." He smiled and continued. "They are not going to turn the boat around for us now. I've been getting by on empty air since this whole ghastly affair started."

"How?" she carried Jojo to a seat and sat her upon her lap. She wanted to hear him talk. Anything to take her mind off the tripods and the horrors of their indiscriminate killing. "I want to enjoy the lull."

He sat beside her and told her of his first encounter with an unseen Martian tripod at Woking station and his waking in the wreckage of the train carriage and the meeting with the train guard.

"How did you come to be with the navy?" she asked.

"I found a local post office and even though it was night, I managed to get the postmaster to send an emergency telegram to the War Office. They have an all-night post office in that part of the City. It was quickly despatched and they replied telling me to go to Southampton and board a coastal defence ship and make sure that land signal stations were being set up along the entire coastline at very short intervals between the regular ones.

"The postmaster got his son to take me to Southampton in a small carriage, which was most kind.

"It's strange really, I was no more than a boring filling clerk and then they sent me on a small errand to Winchester. Afterwards, I find myself in the midst of a most extraordinary adventure—being on board a ship with crewman taking orders from me. I went ashore to get stations set up, but all I really did was tell some signalmen to set up a signal for the passing shipping and to keep in contact with other stations. How they went about it I haven't got a clue. I would go ashore with them, then return when they had their spot. I was going to do the same at your cottage, but events caught up with us."

"I'm glad you showed up when you did. I don't know what I would have done if I was on my own." She squeezed his hand.

He smiled and looked into her eyes. "I suddenly realised how dull my life was when this calamity happened. I dread the thought of going back to being boring old Mister Stanley from the W.O."

"Would it not be a good thing, Albert? All this would no longer be a problem anymore."

"I'm optimistic we will find some way of fighting them, and I long to see one of those tripod things die before my very eyes. I just feel that once one of them goes down, others will follow." He looked down and smiled. "But I still won't go back to being boring Mister Stanley—glorified filling clerk for the War Office. I want to spread my wings and do something else."

"At the moment, everyone's ambition is to survive," she laughed, though she was impressed by his apparent disregard for such terrible things.

"Yes, I agree, and it isn't something that has eluded me, but I just have a gut instinct that the present situation will not prevail. It may get worse, with many trials and tribulations ahead, but something will happen. From out of this desert of madness, there will be a few grains of sanity."

"People pull together and do the most astounding things in a crisis." She looked down and cuddled Jojo, who was nibbling on a biscuit. "It is afternoon now and she hasn't eaten."

"Well, let's see if there is something we can do about it then," said Mister Stanley, standing up. "I'm sure there is something below deck."

Together, they went back down to the lower deck in search of food, while *The Southend Belle* paddled onwards with *HMS Thunder Child* a little off the starboard bow.

Descending the stairway, they entered a companionway and met Ordinary Seaman Lawrence, who beamed with delight at the sight of them.

"Miss Wade and Mister Stanley," he bellowed happily. He looked at little Jojo and said. "And little you."

She giggled and coyly buried her head into Daisy.

"The captain will be pleased to see you, as I just heard him say that he wished he had kept you aboard," continued Lawrence excitedly.

"Really. Now that is most interesting indeed." He looked at Daisy. "I think I had best go and see him." Then back to Lawrence. "Could you help Daisy and Jojo find something to eat while I go to the captain?"

"Of course, Mister Stanley," replied Lawrence, not knowing how to go about it on the paddle steamer, but try he would.

CHAPTER 12

BACK TO THE COASTAL INLAND

The Southend Belle paddled into the Blackwater, her funnel smoking away as she piloted through the other fishing vessels sailing to and fro. Behind, *Thunder Child* followed like an ever-watchful guardian. Her crew had developed a fondness for the little paddle steamer since the escape from Southend.

The coastline, on either side of the estuary, was a hive of activity. Everywhere swarmed with fleeing humanity and anywhere a boat could moor was occupied and, in turn, every vessel was surrounded by rowing boats packed with people. Some even waded and swam about in a desperate bid to get aboard a vessel. The panic was despondent and wherever a person viewed the coastline, there appeared to be incidents of unlawful behaviour where troops and policemen tried to intervene.

Captain McIntosh watched from *Thunder Child*'s bridge, though he was more concerned with getting to Maldon, where the paddle steamer was to take aboard the mysterious French professor.

"How on earth will they find the man among all these refugees?" asked Chudleigh bemused.

"He will be with the authorities at Maldon," replied the captain. "Such as there may be among all this madness."

He abandoned his observation of the northern coastline and looked over the portside, where the estuary cut back southwards at Ramsey Island and the endless line of humanity faded with it. Then his view was blocked by Osea Island as they cruised by an area of land that appeared unoccupied.

"Just around Northey Island, and then we'll be at Maldon, sir," said Chudleigh reassuringly.

"We'll drop anchor before that," McIntosh replied.

"Very good, sir." He thought the captain looked tired and strained. Within a few days, the events had taken their toll and he was sure the unnerving sight of all the refugees along the coastline had started it. The spectacle had become disturbing for all. Then the abandonment of the people on the pier at Southend had bothered the man's conscience further, but there had been nothing he could have done.

McIntosh moved to the voice pipe and called, "Stop all engines."

There was a pause before the orders were relayed down to the engine room. The ironclad stopped as crewmen ran onto the forecastle and unlocked the scattered braces that secured the anchor chains. The capstans started spinning, releasing the shackles that ran out through the hawse pipes—anchors dropped from either side of the bow as the big manacles followed the metal grapnels to the bottom.

"Now we wait for *The Southend Belle* to leave," sighed the Captain.

"And hope no Martians drop in," added Chudleigh.

McIntosh smiled. Chudleigh had a light-hearted way of putting things that he found amusing.

"I want to inspect the gun crews," he added, as though the idea had only recently occurred to him. "Just in case we have gate crashers."

"Well, Captain," began Chudleigh as he followed McIntosh to the back hatch that led to the superstructure. "The old girl might be getting on a bit, but thankfully, her guns are manned by chaps that have had a little practice at using them. As I said before, she's a ship that has been kept out of the way of things and been used for all manner of exercises. One being gunnery, because the top brass didn't give two hoots about scratching the old girl's paint work during lengthy firing practice sessions. Could have done with her when they were blazing away at Alexandria in eighty-two."

"Yes, the shooting there was abysmal, from what I've heard," replied the captain as they walked across the superstructure. He looked over to young Perry, who was standing by Signalman Brandt at the port semaphore. "I'll be at aft or fore turrets if any messages are sent. Get them to me as quick as you can while the starboard messenger lets the bridge know. Understood, lad?"

"Yes, sir," replied Perry, coming to attention and saluting.

The captain moved on, turning to Chudleigh while in motion. "I hope to God our gunners can hit a target if the need arises."

"I'm sure they'll do well, sir. Even with the old girl's muzzle-loaders."

They walked past each funnel, ducking the stress wires securing them to the deck, arriving at the aft part, where they descended the stairway onto the aft turret's roof. A ladder went down the turret's side by the hatchway, where the gun crew were on standby. All stood to attention when the captain and commander entered.

McIntosh looked about, and all seemed to be well. Each gunner was properly dressed and he saw Quartermaster Middleton must have been keeping them all on their toes. He looked down at the metal-grilled floor and the rails the gun carriage moved on. Both the short, stubby barrels stuck out through the gun ports.

He looked to the chief gunner. "Load her. Keep her loaded until I instruct otherwise."

"Yes, sir," replied the gunner. He turned to the rest of the gun crew and barked out his orders as the men went through motions that had become reflex actions. A signal was sent to the deck below where the loading rams went. The gun carriage reversed and the floor revolved until the guns could be tipped—their muzzle bores open before the gutter-like loading rams. A charge came up into each gun barrel and then the floor revolved a little more so the barrels were staring down two more pipes, through which came shells for each barrel. The guns were then raised and the floor again turned until both muzzles could be pushed forward, and back through the gun ports.

"Very good," said McIntosh. "Keep ready at action stations. Don't stand down until the command is given, understood?"

"Yes, sir," replied the chief gunner.

"Good man." The captain left and went along the starboard side of the main deck. He looked in briefly at the wheelhouse and finding that all was well, proceeded to the fore turret, where Fancourt's gun crew would be. He deliberately kept his gaze away from the coastline, where the masses swarmed in search of vessels to take them away from Britain and to the European mainland—a place where the vast majority would never have dreamed of going in their entire lives. It was strange how a small island could rule so much of the planet when so many of its population never left their sanctuary during their entire lifetime.

As they came to the aft turret, Chief Gunner Fancourt was conversing with Quartermaster Middleton. They stood smartly to attention upon the captain's arrival.

McIntosh looked to Fancourt. "Load your guns and keep them loaded. Have your men standing at action stations until you are told to stand down."

"Yes, sir." Fancourt saluted, went into the turret and briskly called the men to action. The guns barrels rolled back inside the gun ports and the hydraulic loading rams could be heard going through the motions.

"Well, Quartermaster," began the captain. "I'd like to see the engine room."

"A pleasure, Captain." The quartermaster smiled confidently. The captain was a leader to his liking and he was eager to accompany the man on his inspection.

Macintosh smiled, liking the demeanour of his quartermaster. He had the ability to be humorous and stern enough to get his men working well. Firm, friendly and fair. Such were good combinations.

He turned to his number one. "Chudleigh, I'd like you to look over the gun crews again. You know them all, so make sure they're ready if needed."

"Very good, sir." He made his way back to the aft turret.

"Well, Quartermaster Middleton. I've yet to see the engine room."

"Much to do in such unusual times, Captain." It was an assumption as he held out his arm in a polite, yet slightly nervous, gesture. After all, he was in front of the captain and didn't want to appear overconfident.

"No, you lead the way," replied McIntosh. "I'll follow."

Middleton smiled agreeably and went to a hatchway along the main deck with the captain on his heels. Inside was a floor hatch with a ladder that led down to the next deck where the officers' mess was located. Beyond was a lower level and though the engines had been stopped, there was still the old familiar noises coming up the ladder way as crewmen went through checks under the supervision of Boatswain Pickles and the chief engineer.

"Captain present," announced Middleton, standing to attention as McIntosh followed down the last few rungs.

"Captain present," called the chief engineer.

All stood rigid as McIntosh nodded his approval and stepped forward.

"Carry on, men," he said, while looking around. He recognised Ordinary Seaman Jolly, obviously under Boatswain Pickles' supervision.

"How are you finding things in the engine room, Jolly?" McIntosh knew his name now. Like young Perry, he was one of the crewmen who had learnt a few things because of his own careless chatter.

Jolly smiled, pleased the Captain remembered him. "Very well, thank you, Captain."

"How on earth did you acquire that injury to your face?"

"I fell down one of the ladder ways, Captain."

McIntosh raised an eyebrow and looked to Boatswain Pickles and then to Middleton. They were all hiding something. Probably some brawl. He sighed. "How's he coming along, Pickles?"

"Splendidly, Captain. Very well indeed, sir."

The captain's nodded, as though he knew more than he was letting on. "Very good. Very good indeed." He looked to the chief engineer. "Any problems with maintenance?"

The chief smiled. "None, Captain. The old girl is tip-top, sir."

McIntosh smiled. "Splendid. Very good indeed." He looked around, nodding at the other engineers who were attending their various functions. He nodded approvingly at each man, then turned to Middleton. "The stokehold next I fancy, Quartermaster."

"Very good, Captain." Middleton gingerly passed him and moved to a stairway on the starboard hull. He looked back. "It's down here, sir."

"Lead on then, Middleton. I'm right behind you." It was a humorous quip and the engineers chuckled. Such small things could put men at their ease. It had the desired effect—even Middleton smiled as he descended the steps.

The stokers were settling due to the ironclad recently weighing anchor, but it was obvious many had only just stopped labouring. Many were covered in coal dust and soaked in sweat, though they all stood rigidly to attention when someone shouted "Captain in the hold."

"At ease, men." The captain was quick to maintain the stoker's short respite. Some still kept the fires going, knowing the lull would probably be brief. The heat was intense and he wondered how the men could bear it for such long periods at a time. He decided the stokehold was truly a horrendous place. Like hell, if viewed from a certain perception and the wretched men that worked in such places weren't envied by other crew members. He looked around at the dirty, blackened faces that stared back as though in fear of him—like he was the devil who put them to work in such infernal surroundings. Then he realised it was the contrast of the whites of their eyes against soot-smeared skin that made them appear so wretched. He felt uncomfortable among them and made his excuses to leave.

Middleton chattered away as they went aft back onto the main deck, where the wind cut across the estuary to refresh him. The respite was only brief, however, as the multitude of refugees made their presence known yet again. McIntosh longed to get back to the bridge, feeling uneasy at the sight.

Middleton followed him up the conning tower, where Perry stood waiting for him to get on deck.

"Captain, signal station reports three tripods heading this way coming over from Foulness Island," Perry blurted out. "The starboard messenger 'as just informed the bridge."

"Good God!" exclaimed the captain. "Did you hear that, Middleton?" He went over to the semaphore and began to ask Brandt questions, while Middleton and Perry followed.

The entire southern side had become frenzied as refugees began to push down to the shoreline. Shots rang out amid the panic, but they did little to calm the mounting hysteria.

"Look, sir," exclaimed Perry to Middleton, while pointing to an inlet beyond Northsea Island. "It's *The Southend Belle.* She's leaving."

The captain had looked around, too. "Let's go to the open bridge and signal from there. If they have the French professor, then we can leave." He looked at Perry. "You come with us, young man, as I will want you to bring a message back to Brandt, which he'll relay to the signal station he's in touch with."

"Yes, sir," replied Perry, pleased to be in on things.

They raced into the bridge where the crew seemed to be a hive of activity. Faulbs stood with Heinemann, chattering over the voice pipe.

"Haul anchor and set engines on standby," called McIntosh.

"Aye, aye, sir."

They went out onto the open bridge where Devour was standing with a lookout man.

"She's leaving already, Captain," said Devour. He was watching the paddle steamer as she came out into the river from Maldon.

"Yes, that was quick. Mind you, her decks are packed. Look!"

"She's signalling, sir," replied Middleton. "The French professor is aboard."

Suddenly, there came a shrill sound that tore across the bay. It was the same noise they had heard at Southend earlier during the day.

"Aloo, aloo, oola."

Booming footsteps rocked the ground as three tripods suddenly appeared above the horizon—each an apocalyptic edifice with ominous off-white trunks that blighted the blue sky. The crescendo of hysteria intensified as a wave of humanity parted on either side of their approach route. They brought a vision of doom. This was to be the way of things.

A fanfare of terror echoed along the opposite coastline as the refugees screamed out in dismay, while the colossal contrivances paid no attention to the human insects that scattered before them. Instead, they appeared to be interested in the boats in the estuary. Especially *the Southend Belle*. It was as though the green compound eyes on each alien structure were transfixed by the paddle steamer.

"God! They're after *The Southend Belle*," exclaimed Devour.

The captain calmly walked inside the bridge, where all were staring in miserable horror at the Martian machines. No one appeared to know what to do and for a moment, he allowed himself time to drink in the sight of the tripods. His observation was broken when young Perry walked backwards into the bridge in open-mouthed surprise.

The boy seaman's terrified gaze didn't dare leave the sight as the three white trunks carried upon thin stilted legs advanced into the River Blackwater. He frowned, wondering why their stilted legs appeared rusty, almost as though they lacked proper maintenance. It was Leutnant Heinemann who unwittingly answered his conjecture.

"That look of corrosion on their legs is some sort of parasitic moss."

Perry began to back away past Lieutenant Faulbs, who was standing by the voice pipe with the same look of abject horror.

Slowly, but with purpose, the tripods waded into the Blackwater—menacingly in pursuit of the paddle steamer. What could *Thunder Child* do? What could anyone do?

Mister Stanley Protects His Loved Ones

The terror aboard *The Southend Belle* was infectious—panic spread amid the new refugees who had boarded at Morden. It had been a quick affair and the paddle steamer had barely docked before it was full and had disembarked. Now, the sight of Foulness Island had wiped the short-lived feelings of relief from the passengers and replaced them with utter dismay. The impending appearance of the three Martian tripods slowly and menacingly wading into the River Blackwater was more than any could stand. Young children screamed, while terrified adults tried to calm them—wishing they could do something about the hopeless plight about to befall them all.

"There, there, pet." Daisy cuddled Jojo into her as the little girl's body began to tremble with fear.

"She senses it from the others," added Mister Stanley as he bent down and cuddled the both of them tightly. "We are going to come through this. Now come with me." His voice was strong and convincing, and Daisy was happy to comply as he pushed his way through people along the upper deck and around the wheelhouse, close to the funnel. Here, he took a rubber ring in case they had to jump into the water.

"There are steps that led down to the bow part over there. It's nearer the water line if we have to jump." He was looking about, his mind ticking over—creating chances and ready to grasp any opportunity.

"I can hear the silence from the shoreline." Daisy was looking back towards Morden, where the masses were standing and watching the events in hopeless open-mouthed silence.

"I think they're as helpless as we are and would love to vent their frustration."

Daisy gulped as the gigantic fighting machines entered the river. "They're definitely after us, Albert. They seem uninterested in the smaller vessels that are scattering."

Mister Stanley took Daisy's hand and led her and little Jojo over to the bulwarks on the port bow. "If it comes to it, this is where we'll jump. Stay clear of the lifeboats and put Jojo in the ring once we're in the water."

"Why not use the lifeboats?" she asked fearfully.

"Because they're big and those things are going for people. A crowd in a lifeboat will be a tempting target." He turned to the tripods still some distance away, yet gaining all the time. "Those things have no compassion for our kind. We're like vermin to them—pests that must be eradicated."

"Do you really think that's how they view us, Albert?"

He looked to her sorrowfully. "I'm afraid I do, Daisy, and we must learn how to be as equally detached in killing them. Whatever means we can muster, we must use. No matter how terrifying or horrific." Again he turned as the machine creatures waded closer—his heart skipping a beat while he allowed the fear to pollute his body like a coloured mist in clear liquid. It settled and became constant as all aboard *The Southend Belle* held their breath in fear.

Suddenly, there was a whooping sound from *HMS Thunder Child* and as all aboard the paddle steamer turned to look at the valiant little ironclad, they saw froth and foam churning from the vessel's stern as the propellers kicked into action.

Those upon the shoreline reacted as though awakened from a trance and began cheering hysterically.

Mister Stanley looked from the ironclad to shore and then to the tripods. His excitement grew and a surge of adrenaline was coursing through his veins. "My God," he muttered excitedly and shaking his head in disbelief. "They're going to engage them," he muttered ecstatically.

"Are you sure?" Daisy hoped with all her desire that he was right.

"Yes, I'm positive."

From the shoreline, there came a rhythmic chanting like a crowd at a football or rugby match cheering for their side. Except there had to be upwards of a hundred thousand people upon the northern river bank. The roar became colossal and for a moment, the gigantic tripods seemed to shrivel within the roaring aura. It was almost as though they hesitated before entering a monumental arena. Something different from the usual way of things— a new experience—one that was unexpected.

"Stay by the rails and pray, Daisy," he said as he cuddled her close with little Jojo in the middle. "We will get through this. One way or another—by hook or by crook—we will do it."

"I believe you, Albert. I really do." She put her head against his chest and prayed.

Battle of the Blackwater

So these were Martians! The tripod fighting machines that could bring destruction and death with their heat-rays and black poisonous smoke. Giant insect like armoured mechanisms, inside of each an alien or aliens. Monstrous, spiderlike legs that carried an armoured trunk high above the ground—a hundred feet, maybe more.

Thunder Child's crew had gasped in horror as the gigantic machine creatures strode across Foulness, their steps booming across the estuary and growing louder with each thunderous crash. The pandemonium suddenly died when the sea-water muffled their steps. The enormous monstrosities began to wade into the tributary as they pursued *The Southend Belle*, which was packed with refugees. All three monstrosities waded deeper in pursuit while the people on board screamed in terror. Their cries fanned out across the quiescent sea.

Upon the further shore, from Maldon to the Naze, a stream of humanity watched in horror—silent for the helpless ones on board.

None of the Royal Navy vessels, save *Thunder Child*, were in the estuary, and the dread of thousands gathered along the coastline could be felt among the entire crew.

"Good God!" exclaimed Faulbs. "It's going for *The Southend Belle*."

Captain McIntosh gritted his teeth as reason clicked quickly into motion. He allowed himself a brief gaze at the other launches and smacks that made for the open sea. Then his attention returned to the tripod creatures that neared the paddle steamer with alarming speed.

He had the helpless multitude as his audience; the valiant ironclad with its obsolete guns and his stout-hearted men. His bold crew would have to be knights in shining armour.

"According to reports, tripods have been brought down by cannon fire, if accurate," he said aloud.

Quartermaster Middleton smiled. "Indeed, Captain."

Dark memories of the pier at Southend returned. It haunted them all. They had obeyed orders. Should they do it again?

All took another look at the helpless women and children packed on the open deck of the fleeing paddle steamer, allowing the sight of terrified parents cuddling their crying infants to burn deep into each sailor's conscience.

No!

Not this time.

"Red one ten. Then full ahead," yelled the captain. The die was cast and determined faces were locked in grim acceptance, glad of the commitment. They were also frightened, but more of watching the helpless people on the paddle steamer than of confronting the Martians. *Thunder Child* would engage the abominations. No more running! Now they would take the fight to the intruders.

Perry grabbed the hatch door as the ironclad turned sharply to port—his heart thumping as the bridge became alive with activity. It was as though he was an infant watching adults do the thing they did best. He was mesmerised as the brave men before him began to function in unison and his heart was thumping with a passionate and patriotic pride. For a moment, he was among the valiant knights as *Thunder Child* ploughed through the waters towards titan hosts.

"Green five," barked the captain, adjusting the bow's ram slightly as *Thunder Child* proceeded to her destiny.

"Green five," yelled Faulbs down the voice pipe.

"I want guns targeted on the one at the extreme left, while we ram the right. We'll worry about the centre one after." Captain McIntosh was resigned to the fight and everyone could feel the blood pumping through their veins as the fear and excitement mixed a lethal cocktail of adrenaline that made each man ache to scream with rage.

The crew turned and looked to the northern bank as a thunderous applause rippled from the crowded shore. The audience of refugees screamed their approval. A vast horde, clapping and cheering in the most British of spirits—the likes of which had never been heard before. Suddenly, the entire estuary had become a gladiatorial arena.

Quartermaster Middleton stood beside Perry. "All right, lad?"

"Yes, Quartermaster," he replied fiercely.

"Good, lad," replied the old seaman enthusiastically. There was a passionate glint in his eyes and young Perry's manner was to his liking. "Hear that shoreline, lad. A tide of humanity rippling with adulation and screaming for us."

Perry began to feel the adrenaline rush as the chanting fanned out across the estuary..."*THUNDER CHILD, THUNDER CHILD.*"

"Let the show begin," muttered Middleton. "Now is our moment, lad." He winked at Perry and walked off to the front hatch, then out onto the open bridge again, where, before him, the looming tripods had stopped. They grew larger as *Thunder Child* cut a course towards them.

Perry was redundant and no one seemed interested in him. He should have gone back out to the signalman. He would in a moment, but for now, he could not tear his gaze from the Martians. He barely noticed as *Thunder Child* sliced the retreating paddle steamer's wake and pointed her bow towards one of the tripods—so deep in the sea, the alien's legs were all but immersed.

"*THUNDER CHILD, THUNDER CHILD.*"

Their protective trunks were just above the water line, where disgusting compound globes protruded from each casing. Perry couldn't make out whether they were organic parts of the Martians, or window components of their protective armour. Like giant fly heads with their tubes upon movable flexes resembling antenna.

"*THUNDER CHILD, THUNDER CHILD.*"

Suddenly, each machine halted as though astounded or puzzled by *Thunder Child*'s brazen advance.

"*THUNDER CHILD, THUNDER CHILD.*"

"Steady and hold fire until I give the command." McIntosh raised his binoculars while the order was barked out again through the voice pipe.

"They don't know what to make of us, sir," said Faulbs.

The captain dropped his glasses and gritted his teeth. "We're going to get one of you blighters at least," he hissed.

"*THUNDER CHILD, THUNDER CHILD.*"

Middleton came back inside, acting as though he was on a routine gun drill. He was the only person to appear oblivious of the hostile abnormalities as *Thunder Child* cruised closer. "Guns in position, Captain."

"*THUNDER CHILD, THUNDER CHILD.*"

Perry couldn't help noticing how calm and professional everyone was as they charged into the jaws of destruction—ominous arms that poised to engulf them.

"*THUNDER CHILD, THUNDER CHILD.*"

"Very good, Quartermaster. Hold steady until I give the order. They're inquisitive. Let's milk that fact if we can." The captain was a picture of steadfast confidence.

"Curiosity killing the cat," muttered Faulbs in agreement.

"*THUNDER CHILD, THUNDER CHILD.*"

Suddenly, one of the tripod's cylinders raised upwards on its flex. How, none could say, except the cord must have had some sort of artificial spine. Everyone braced themselves and Perry thought his heart had skipped a beat, but the steady voice of Captain McIntosh abated them.

"Hold fire and maintain course," he ordered.

At that very moment, a canister shot from the cylinder of the tripod. It hit the bow of the ship and bounced into the sea spewing black smoke.

"*THUNDER CHILD, THUNDER CHILD.*"

"Put masks on," ordered the captain and instantly, they all pulled wet handkerchiefs wrapped around chunks of coal over their mouths.

Perry was aghast, they were still charging towards the Martians, who began taking tentative steps backwards—unsure what to make of them.

"*THUNDER CHILD, THUNDER CHILD.*"

"Steady," yelled the Captain.

"Fore turret has target plum in sight, Captain," yelled someone excitedly.

"Fire," shouted the captain in the same instant one of the tripods discharged a flash of light. There was a boom as *Thunder Child*'s guns roared and a screech as the alien heat-ray ripped through the bow. The ship shuddered and Perry lunged forward against the standard compass, colliding with Lieutenant Faulbs as the halyard erupted in a ball of flame and twisted metal. Hitting the deck, he looked up through the bridge window as one of the tripod's trunks erupted—flame and blooded gore, red, like human plasma, burst from the ruptured casing as a high-pitched shriek tore through the air. The colossal edifice rocked unsteadily against the blue sky.

Meanwhile, the remaining tripods turned their trunks and watched as their stricken comrade toppled into the sea.

Small arms fire serenaded the triumphant cheering and variously placed six-pound guns sang out in defiance. Most were scattered along the guardrail of the superstructure and out on the open bridge.

Perry got onto his hands and knees, dazed from his violent knock. He looked outside the open hatch to the rear of the bridge, his ears ringing, just as both funnels lifted off the deck like rockets—the stress wires snapping and pinging through the air under the strain of the explosive force. It was as though he was watching it all through tunnel vision and everything was happening slowly.

He saw Brandt decapitated as the wire cut through the air—a razor edged whip hissing out, slicing the hull of one of the lifeboats. Two balls of flame spewed up from the gaping holes that were left by the launched funnels and the starboard signalman smashed lifeless beside the inferno as though the sky was about to rain dead crewmen. Then, through the madness of orange-tongued flame like a banshee from hell, emerged the German liaison officer, Heinemann. His face contorted with rage as he fired over the bulwarks at the alien enemy, screaming at the top of his voice, though Perry couldn't hear what he was saying. It was as the faint feeling swept over him the shell of silence burst, allowing the sound of mayhem to flood his draining consciousness that he finally made out the words.

"They can die. They can..." The soothing blackness claimed him as another explosion tore up the halyard, pounding the upper fore turret and ripping into the bridge.

"Get up now, lad, look lively," yelled Pickles as he lifted Jolly. The engine room was still intact, despite the hissing steam leaking from various parts of ruptured piping. All around, engineers were gathering their jumbled wits, aiding one another. "Get to that engine throttle and hold the last ordered position. I think the bridge has gone, but we're on a ramming course." He pointed Jolly to the starboard engine throttle while going to the portside.

A booming echo bounded from the bow and along the hull past the destroyed stokeholds as the ship jolted violently. Jolly smashed into the engine throttle as the sound of cheering came aft, followed by a second alien screech—like that of a giant wounded bird.

"We've rammed one," yelped Jolly, as the sound of the Martian tripod scraped along the outside of the starboard hull. Intensified small arms fire could be heard amid excited shouts from sailors, no doubt, firing over the starboard bulwark into the sea where the floundering creature had fallen.

Pickles looked up the ladder way that led out. "I'm sure that's the second one at least, Jolly. I heard them cheering from the steering position. They were shouting as the guns went off."

"And the lids of the stokeholds blew. The stokers, Bosun! What about them poor bastards?" Jolly ran to the stairway that led down, but stopped as he peered below into the scattered coals that glowed around the smouldering corpses of the stokers.

The boatswain called to him, as he stood mesmerised. "Come on, Jolly lad. Get yourself aft." He turned to all the engineers about him. "Every man aft. I repeat, every man aft."

There was a scramble for the ladder at first, but it was quickly quelled as the leading engineer fired some home-grown discipline into them. "Stop right there, you bunch of babbling tarts," he yelled. "We're doing this like a routine training exercise and I want no bloody wingers. Now proceed and properly, or you'll be sent to the back." An orderly line formed and the seriously wounded were put to the front with able-bodied men helping them up.

Pickles went to Jolly, who lingered at the top of the stairway. Before him, the lower levelled stoke-hold began to burn more furiously—the heat forced him to take a step back. He lowered his head help-lessly. He could do nothing for the stokers who had been killed during the explosion from the heat-ray.

"Come on, lad," said Pickles. "There's nothing you can do for them poor sods. They're done for. Come on now, let's get out."

They joined the line that was rapidly shrink-ing as each man scrambled up the ladder way to the next deck. Just as Jolly began to climb with the stout-hearted chief engineer behind, there came the gushing sound of the sea tearing into the stoke-hold and the noise of hissing steam as the burning coal embers were doused.

"Christ, she's going," muttered the chief engi-neer. "Quick, boy, up you go."

Jolly scrambled up to the next deck and turned to look down as the chief engineer followed. Behind him, Pickles started to climb, but was swept away from the ladder by the onrush of seawater.

"Bosun!" yelled Jolly as the engineer climbed past him. He was about to go down, but was pulled back by others. The floor hatch was shut and clamped down, while Jolly protested furiously for the chance to aid Boatswain Pickles. He was smashed against the wall by one man and another barked orders at him.

"Proceed up to the main deck. Bosun Pickles is lost and that's that. The ship's sinking and this crew must buy as much time as they can."

The boatswain had been sacrificed and as Jolly climbed up to the next deck, he visualised the wretched fellow drowning in the claustrophobic darkness—kicking and spluttering in futility for a last breath, in the terrifying knowledge that the inevitable was upon him. Abandoned and left to his fate by hard disciplined men who would bleed later, when it was too late. Yet always knowing they would do the same again.

He clenched his teeth as his eyes watered. Never had he felt such pity, and it hurt him deeply that he could do nothing for the doomed boatswain. As he made his way aft, he made a vow that he would survive this day. He had to be strong; he would be firm and live. This hurt was important and he would bear it to his dying day.

Sailors staggered about the main deck, lowering lifeboats amid the roar of flames that engulfed the bow and upon the superstructure's deck. Gunner Fancourt swayed as he emerged from the forward gun turret, coughing from the effect of the smoke. The rest of the gun crew were dead, he being the only survivor from the eruption that ripped up the halyard. It was as much as he could do to stand and he tried to gulp in the clearer air, but the heat from the burning forecastle caused him to retch violently.

Most of the crew were making for the stern and the ship was drifting helpless in the surrounding smoke. A couple of rifle shots briefly brought him to his senses. He looked up where the superstructure burned, to see Heinemann pointing his gun down the starboard side of the ship, still plugging away at the second vanquished Martian. He chuckled—the young German officer amused him. The man was blind with rage and shooting rounds into the alien flotsam and jetsam was the only way to abate it.

A reassuring hand was put around him as his legs buckled and the comforting sound of Lieutenant Devour rekindled his ebbing strength.

"Come now," said the French officer. "Not now, Mr Fancourt. Not after the bold stand you made. Come, we will get away from this dying lady and you'll remember her kindly in future days."

Beneath a blackened face caked in congealed blood, Fancourt smiled. "Do you really think so, sir?"

Devour smiled. "I know so, Mr Fancourt. We are leaving with the rest of these men." He looked up at Heinemann. "You might want to come down now, my friend. Help me with this man who put a shell into the first tripod."

Heinemann looked down and smiled as the manic glint in his eyes died. Reason surfaced and he left the guardrail, while Devour and Fancourt gingerly walked along the starboard side of the main deck. As they passed the steering position's hatchway, the young German emerged and supported Fancourt from the other side. The two foreign officers made their way to the stern with him, where the remnants of the crew congregated.

Some gunners were shouting around the rear turret, which was still operational. They had carried a couple shells from the deck below because the loading rams were out of action.

"There's another one out in that black mist somewhere and it would be nice if the bastard showed up in front of the barrels loaded with these babies," said one of the men, still full of spirit.

"Christ, ain't they had enough?" scolded Fancourt.

Heinemann laughed. "Oh, if the boys want to fight, you have to let them."

They got into a lifeboat packed with dazed and blackened crewmen, then pulled away as *Thunder*

Child listed slightly on her portside. They watched on as she drifted away, burning and belching thick fumes from the bow and the once funnelled super-structure. They left one area of thick smoke and pro-ceeded into another fog, which had been left by the Martians. They began to check their handkerchiefs, while some made desperate attempts to find another for Fancourt, who had lost his when the turret was engulfed in flames from the heat-ray's explosion.

Commander Chudleigh was inside the aft turret where the gun crew were loading the shells into the gun muzzles excitedly. He'd ordered the others to go below and bring the shells up on learning the hydraulic loading rams were down. His voice was muffled, due to the coal-stained handkerchief over his mouth and, like the rest of the crew, looked almost comical with his blackened face.

"The other is port," he said. "I'm positive of it."

The turret began to revolve as the chief gunner called to the sailors outside. "Get out of the line of fire," he roared to the crewman on the port quar-ter. The fleeing deck hands scattered as instructed, while the rest of the gun crew observed from the gun ports, scrutinising the mist—looking for a sign of the third tripod.

An alien cry rang out from the black fog—long, drawn out—allowing the, by now, trembling gun crew to know it was waiting to emerge and strike when the opportunity presented itself.

"Keep a sharp look, men, and don't forget they move quickly and are intelligent."

"If that one's so smart, why is it letting us know its rough whereabouts by groaning, Commander?" The chief gunner was baffled.

Chudleigh's eyes widened. "Very good, man. Turn to starboard."

All the gun crew stared in amazement, as though unsure they had heard him right.

"Do it right now, damn it," he barked furiously. "I've never been more serious in all my life. And keep your eyes well and truly peeled, is that understood?"

"Yes, sir," came the collective response. He had charged them with his firm manner and all at once, they believed he could be right. The Martian might be trying to trick them.

Again the chief gunner screamed out at the fleeing deck hands on the starboard quarter. "Get out of the line of fire. Guns coming about." The response was immediate as sailors parted for the line of fire. "Right, lad, watch for the birdie and we might end up bagging three of the bastards with us still not out."

Beads of perspiration began to form on Chudleigh's forehead as he waited nervously with the gun crew. It had to be circling for a starboard attack, that's why it had made a noise on the port. He gritted his teeth—supposing it went to the bow. The ship was finished there. No! It couldn't know that, even if *Thunder Child* was hit there, the alien would think the ship's punch was here, because of its eyewitness account—seeing two felled comrades. Outside, the rest of the crew were abandoning ship, but he and the rest of the men in the turret were determined to wait just that little bit longer.

His eyes opened to the sound of screaming that tore through the blackness, pulling him into the conscious world where heat and thick smoke filled the bridge. Lieutenant Faulbs sat dead, his back against the ship's pelorus and voice pipe—his vacant eyes stared in open-mouthed surprise at the photograph of Queen Victoria, the frame dangling irregularly upon the wall.

"Perry, are you alright?" It was the strained voice of Quartermaster Middleton somewhere within the smoke.

"Yes, sir, what happened?"

"We've been hit, lad. Can you move?"

Perry turned onto his stomach and was about to stand, when he was advised against it. "The smoke's too thick, boy. Crawl to the hatch and abandon ship. Do you hear?"

"Yes, sir. Are you coming too?"

"No, just get out now. Come on, lad, quick as you can."

From outside in every direction, the sound of complete pandemonium was heard as roaring flames intensified. He began gingerly crawling to the hatchway as the ship started to list—for a moment, parting the smoke—where he caught sight of Quartermaster Middleton lying beneath the wreckage of twisted steel before the observation window. The whole front was simply ripped inwards and the wretched man was trapped beneath the debris. Through the gaping hole where shredded metal looked like torn paper, the bow was ablaze, with the surrounding steel glowing from the vehement heat. Beyond was a thick, black alien fog that had been seeping from the strange canister, fired before the battle had commenced.

"Get out, boy, we're finished!" screamed the Quartermaster again.

Ignoring the order, Perry doggedly crawled towards him, past the lifeless Captain McIntosh, who was slumped against the ruptured piping, still clasping his binoculars and retaining the same calm expression in death as he had during the attack. He finally reached the injured man, who was coughing from the effects of thickening smoke.

"There's nothing you can do, lad. Go, for Christ sake. She's finished."

Perry still partially dazed, replied, "We got one of them though, sir. Didn't we?"

"Two, boy, we've rammed the second while you were dazed, but there's still one more out in the smoke, so get out now. She's sinking—there's not much time."

Again, he ignored the old seaman—a strict disciplinarian who, until this day, he would never have dared to disobey—but to leave the man in such circumstances was beyond him. Grabbing part of the bent iron window frame and using it as a crude lever, he heaved upwards with all his might. The tangled debris squealed in protest and somehow, the Quartermaster was able to pull himself free, despite his broken leg.

Pleased with his efforts, Perry grinned. "It's not over yet, sir." His face was covered in dust and clotted blood smeared his forehead. He began to pull the officer towards the hatchway, while far off beyond the dying ship's fire and smoke, out in the unearthly mist came the shrill scream of their enemy. It was difficult to fathom, almost like grating metal combined with the high-pitched screech of some gigantic bird.

It rang out hauntingly and for a moment, the survivors were silent, chilled by the thought of being helpless and waiting for the final onslaught. The aft gun fired defiantly in reply, heartening many. After all, they had brought two of the tripod beasts crashing to the sea; perhaps they could claim another of the Martian monsters.

"They might get that one too, sir," yelled Perry excitedly, above the inferno continuing to rage. Once again as though on cue, shouts of panic-stricken seamen were heard as he pulled the quartermaster out past the twisted metal, onto the open bridge's overhanging deck and down the ladder way that led to the top of the fore turret burning from within—the intense heat forced them to move quickly to the turret's side ladder which led down to the main deck.

"It'll be no use, lad, another will come. Believe me, it's like spitting in the wind."

The ship tilted more violently to port, toppling them from the ladder when they were halfway down. Middleton cursed his confounded luck as the pain from his broken leg racked his entire body. Perry pulled him up, while about them the deck was unrecognisable due to the devastation and fires.

"I'll get us to a lifeboat."

"No, boy! We'll go straight into the water." He grasped Perry's arms wanting to impress the urgency upon him. "Those things don't care about conventions. A lifeboat will be another target. Let's take our chances swimming. In this cloud, we'll be obscured and our prospects will be better, the Essex coast is just a little way off."

Another shell boomed defiantly from the stern sending the projectile into the inky haze where the third Martian tripod was suspected to be lurking. There was an explosion followed by a shrill screech and instantly, a ray of light shot back in reply into the rear of the quarterdeck, where a colossal explosion shook the craft from stern to bow, lifting both men and slamming them to the deck; all about, timbers crashed and metal buckled. Stressed steel wires snapped around the lookout mast and whipped through the air, while smaller explosions shook within the ship from the keel upwards.

"That's the aft turret gone. She's helpless now! We've not got much time, boy. She's a goner," yelled the quartermaster.

"We're out of here then, sir." Perry supported him and had no choice but to go the way the vessel listed. They flung themselves overboard, but fell only a short distance before hitting the sea. The impact was fiercer than expected due to their life jackets resisting the drop deeper into the icy depths.

Instantly, they were lifted by a wave as both gasped for air. The sudden heat was replaced by the cold sea, which caused a further shock to their already stressed systems.

Middleton called out. "Swim for it! Get as far away from the ship as possible."

Perry swam for all he was worth, determined to be clear of the suction when *Thunder Child* sank and was heartened to catch glimpses of the quartermaster keeping up with him, despite his broken limb. Survival mustered a physical durability in the man's determination, and Perry couldn't help admiring such spirit. Determinedly, they battled against the waves with great desire to survive the abominations they had faced and to escape the inevitable demise of the valiant ironclad that had served them magnificently, achieving more than any could have expected.

Fresh explosions fanned out across the sea as both stopped to watch *Thunder Child*'s final moment. There was the bellow of protesting iron as it buckled under the sea's pressure—surrendering to the water's hissing legion of bubbling effervescence that danced up and burst with wicked delight—gathering the noble ironclad and pulling it down to its murky base.

"Keep swimming. Don't stop, lad," yelled the quartermaster, bringing him to his senses.

He was about to resume when suddenly, a light shone through the uncanny smog and the form of a lifeboat could be made out approaching them.

"Ahoy there," called a voice from the advancing craft.

"No," hissed the quartermaster. "Take no notice. The other thing will get them. It's another target. Swim for it. Don't stop! Go it alone, boy."

Something in the urgency of the man's voice convinced him that he should persist in his own efforts, and the realisation that the other Martian tripod was still in the vicinity edged him in favour of the quartermaster's advice. He began to thrust his arms forward with purposeful strokes making more progress towards the obscured coastline. He must have been swimming for a couple of minutes when he heard Middleton's distant protests from behind and stopped to see what the confusion was about. The lifeboat had drawn up alongside the man and in frustration, he was trying to convince the crew that he didn't want to get on board.

"Come on, sir, we'll soon have you out of there and on dry land," said a friendly voice.

"Leave off, will you? Go your own way if you want to stay in that thing. You're just another target floating in the vicinity where two of them have been destroyed by us."

"He's a bit delirious, Sid. Give us a hand to drag him aboard, will you? There's another poor sod over there."

"No, blast you. We're going it alone."

"Come on now, Quartermaster, let's 'ave yer…"

"No, leave me alone." Middleton cursed and fought with the lifeboat crew, who grappled back, trying to haul him out of the water.

Perry watched in horror; behind, the soot-like nebula became more transparent and the ghostly form of a Martian tripod's armoured body appeared. He couldn't be sure, but the creature seemed to have sustained some sort of injury. There was red plasma running down the side of its white armour wrapping. Its long legs were submerged, and it seemed its protective trunk was hovering just above the waves. The two luminous green orbs protruding from the front of the casing glowed within the mist basking the area with radiance.

There followed an eerie silence as the quartermaster froze in the clutches of the lifeboat crew, half in and out of the water. His unwelcome rescuers, sensing the sudden change, lingered and slowly turned to confront the cause his abrupt lack of ardour.

"Blimey, it's come back," one of them had time to mutter.

A small cylinder lifted above the armoured body upon the creature's flexible pipes to point down at the boat. There came a victorious high-pitched cry from the metal monster that tore out through the black mist, followed by a blinding flash of light as the heat-ray swooped down on the boat. A wicked and extravagant ball of flame dilated, which devoured the tiny vessel before splinters and twisted bodies were spewed forth in all directions.

Like a spider returning to its lair, the encased monster sank back into the mist with only its eyes visible—huge, green compound spheres staring at Perry as though unsure what to make of him. Gradually, they too, faded, though the lone sailor was loath to move for several more minutes, just allowing himself to float, shocked with the memory of those dazzling globes that had stayed to watch over the carnage.

There had been the sight and sound of thousands screaming from the shoreline—now there was nothing but a surrounding mist and an eerie silence. No one from the lifeboat had survived, including Quartermaster Middleton, whose life he had momentarily saved—so the man might, during a brief reprieve, save his. The icy sea was just bearable and he was concerned as to whether or not he could make it. After a while, he continued in his exertions towards the coast, where the entire country was said to be running alive with such monstrosities. Sneezing, he thought a minor cold was the least of his worries compared to what the future held in store as he sluggishly swam into the mist—towards the northern shoreline that he hoped would be beyond.

The Gratitude of Mister Stanley

The black alien mist dispersed over the now quiet scene. Hundreds of thousands of people along the shoreline were stunned into silence as they gawked in amazement at what had happened before their very eyes. The paddle steamer's desperate refugees looked on in amazement, feeling the angry silence spread over the desolate waters, where only flotsam bobbed upon the rolling waves.

What everyone had witnessed had been truly awe-inspiring—beyond belief—and yet it had happened, right before all.

"*Thunder Child* is gone," whispered Daisy, holding her hand to her mouth. "All those brave young men."

"They took three tripods with them." Mister Stanley was visibly overwhelmed by such bravery. "They did it for us. I saw its guns hit one and ram another, but there was still cannon fire from within the black mist. They must have taken the third."

All around, there began mutterings of approval from the paddle steamer's passengers and upon the shoreline, people began a slow clap that grew in intensity and as that began to build, an enthusiastic chanting was discerned.

"*Thunder Child, Thunder Child*, we will always love you, *Thunder Child*." It began to echo out from along the entire shoreline east of Maldon and descend upon the River Blackwater. A homage that would ring out in eternity—never to die, for such tales could not be allowed to. "*Thunder Child, Thunder Child*, we will always love you *Thunder Child*."

Daisy stood up and clenched Mister Stanley's hand, encouraging him to respond. He smiled his approval and stood up, stroking Jojo's cheek, which immediately calmed the infant. She rewarded him with a big smile.

"They do die, Albert. There must be other ways to kill the devilish monsters."

"There will be other things, Daisy. You mark my words."

They looked into each other's eyes and smiled. "In such a short time we have been through a great deal together, Albert." Her eyes began to water. "I feel as though I've always known you."

"The same applies to me, Daisy." He looked out over the Blackwater. "It's as though all this was meant to happen and I was always meant to meet you through this."

Suddenly, little Jojo burst through their serene moment of affection and sneezed. An explosion of mucus from her little nose caused her to whimper.

"Oh my dear," said Mister Stanley, producing a handkerchief. "Maybe those nasty Martians could catch such a horrendous cold, aye, little one?" He smiled and wiped her nose clean and again he was rewarded with a kindly smile from the little girl as she cuddled into Daisy Wade, feeling safe in her caring arms.

The eerie quiet had gone amid a fanfare of chanting people. Thousands and thousands of people who didn't know whether they would still be alive tomorrow. But for now, they were happy and would enjoy the respite while it lasted. Meanwhile, *The Southend Belle* paddled eastwards out into the open sea.

"I still don't want to get aboard one of those foreign bound ships, Albert." There was a look of concern in Daisy.

"I've fixed it so we'll stay aboard this vessel. We'll be going backwards and forwards for some time, no doubt, but we won't be too far from the coastline."

EPILOGUE

It was 1903 and Jojo was approaching seven. She had been looking forward to the gathering all week and could barely contain herself with the excitement. Her foster mother, Daisy, had bought her a new dress for the occasion and her hair was in ringlets.

"Do you think there will be lots of people, Mummy?" As they approached Herne Bay's town hall, she became more anxious.

"Of course, pet. I've told you on at least a dozen occasions now," she replied jovially.

Albert Stanley smiled at the little girl. How she had grown and what joy she had brought to his wife, Daisy, and himself. The girl looked up at him.

"Do you think so too, Daddy?"

"Oh I most certainly do, Jojo. I know that Mr Lawrence will be there for a fact and he said he's going to bring along three very special people for us to meet."

"Who is Mister Lawrence?" Her cute inquisitive voice made them bubble with excited joy.

Daisy laughed. "He was the young seaman with your dad when we were all hiding in the coal bunker. The one in the backyard."

They approached the main doorway and were ushered in amid smiles and polite gestures to the main hall where the banquet seemed to be in full swing. There were people gossiping in scattered throngs and reliving old memories.

"Mister Stanley." The respectful call contained a hint of excitement and, as all three turned, they saw a young suited man approaching with three sailors behind.

"My word, its Mister Lawrence," yelped Albert Stanley, filled with glee. "Well I never. I take it you are out of the navy then."

"Only just," laughed Lawrence as he held his hand out to Daisy. "So pleased to meet you again…"

"I'm Mrs Stanley now," she beamed and looked down. "And this is little Jojo."

His eyes lit up with enchanted surprise. "Oh splendid. Absolutely splendid." He looked to the little girl. "I bet you don't remember me, do you?"

Jojo looked up with a smile. "No, but I have heard of you," she replied politely.

Lawrence looked up to Daisy and Albert Stanley. "Oh I can't say how pleased I am for you all, Mister and Mrs Stanley."

"Oh please, call me Albert," replied Mister Stanley.

"My pleasure, and do call me Robert."

Daisy smiled. "I would like you to call me Daisy."

All were now on familiar terms with one another and with handshakes and well-wishes quickly dispensed with, Robert Lawrence turned to the three sailors behind him.

"May I take this opportunity to present three very special men?" He held a hand back as the three seamen moved forward. "Signalman Perry, Able Seaman Jolly and Gunner Fancourt. Very special men who were formerly crew of *HMS Thunder Child* during the Battle of the Blackwater."

The three sailors smiled, allowing Albert and Daisy to make a monumental fuss of them. They were led to the refreshment counter and their plates were filled. They were then taken to a quiet corner, where Albert and Daisy heaped more praise upon them. It was not long before they were listening to the saga of each sailor's view of the battle, and how each had managed to escape from the sinking vessel.

Printed in Great Britain
by Amazon